Dedalus European Cl⟨
General Editor: Mike Mitchell

The Maimed

Hermann Ungar

The Maimed

Translated by Mike Mitchell

Dedalus

Published in the UK by Dedalus Ltd, Langford Lodge, St Judith's Lane, Sawtry,
Cambs, PE28 5XE
email: DedalusLimited@compuserve.com
www.dedalusbooks.com

ISBN 1 903517 10 9

Dedalus is distributed in the United States by SCB Distributors,
15608 South New Century Drive, Gardena, California 90248
email: info@scbdistributors.com   web site: www.scbdistributors.com

Dedalus is distributed in Australia & New Zealand by Peribo Pty Ltd,
58 Beaumont Road, Mount Kuring-gai N.S.W. 2080
email: peribo@bigpond.com

Dedalus is distributed in Canada by Marginal Distribution,
Unit 102, 277 George Street North, Peterborough, Ontario, KJ9 3G9
email: marginal@marginalbook.com   web site: www.marginal.com

Dedalus is distributed in Italy by Apeiron Editoria & Distribuzione,
Localita Pantano, 00060 Sant'Oreste (Roma)
email: grt@apeironbookservice.com   web site: apeironbookservice.com

First published in Germany in 1923
First English translation in 2002

The Maimed translation copyright © Mike Mitchell 2002

The right of Mike Mitchell to be identified as the translator of this work has been
asserted by him in accordance with the Copyright, Designs and Patents Act, 1988.

Typeset by RefineCatch Ltd
Printed in Finland by WS Bookwell

A C.I.P. listing for this book is available on request.

THE AUTHOR

Hermann Ungar (1893–1929) was a German-speaking Jew from Moravia who was active as a writer in Berlin and Prague in the 1920s. Critics spoke of him in the same breath as Kafka, and he was feted in France after the publication of the translation of *The Maimed* in 1928.

After the war he was forgotton in Germany, despite praise from individual writers, but the reissue of the French translation in 1987 was again greeted with enthusiastic reviews: "Hermann Ungar is a great writer, unique . . . No history of literature should ignore his works."

THE TRANSLATOR

Mike Mitchell is one of Dedalus's editorial directors and is responsible for the Dedalus translation programme. His publications include *The Dedalus Book of Austrian Fantasy, Peter Hacks: Drama for a Socialist Society* and *Austria* in the *World Bibliographical Series*.

Mike Mitchell's translations include all the novels of Gustav Meyrink, three by Herbert Rosendorfer, *The Great Bagarozy* by Helmut Krausser and *Simplicissimus* by Grimmelshausen; his latest is *Poems and Plays* by Oskar Kokoschka.

His translation of Rosendorfer's *Letters Back to Ancient China* won the 1998 Schegel-Tieck German Translation Prize.

German Literature from Dedalus

Dedalus features German Literature in translation in its programme of contemporary and classic European fiction and in its anthologies.

Androids from Milk – Eugen Egner £7.99
Undine – Fouqué £6.99
Simplicissimus – J. J. C. Grimmelshausen £10.99
The Life of Courage – J. J. C. Grimmelshausen £6.99
The Great Bagarozy – Helmut Krausser £7.99
The Other Side – Alfred Kubin £9.99
The Road to Darkness – Paul Leppin £7.99
The Angel of the West Window – Gustav Meyrink £9.99
The Golem – Gustav Meyrink £6.99
The Green Face – Gustav Meyrink £6.99
The Opal (& other stories) – Gustav Meyrink £7.99
Walpurgisnacht – Gustav Meyrink £6.99
The White Dominican – Gustav Meyrink £6.99
The Architect of Ruins – Herbert Rosendorfer £8.99
Letters Back to Ancient China – Herbert Rosendorfer £9.99
Stefanie – Herbert Rosendorfer £7.99
The Maimed – Hermann Ungar £6.99

Anthologies featuring German Literature in translation:
The Dedalus Book of Austrian Fantasy – editor M. Mitchell £10.99
The Dedalus Book of German Decadence – editor R. Furness £9.99
The Dedalus Book of Surrealism – editor M. Richardson £9.99
Myth of the World: Surrealism 2 – editor M. Richardson £9.99
The Dedalus Book of Medieval Literature – editor B. Murdoch £9.99

Forthcoming titles include:
Tearaway – J. J. C. Grimmelshausen £6.99
The Class – Hermann Ungar £8.99

FOREWORD

After the publication of his second novel, *Die Klasse* (The Class), in 1927, the main Viennese newspaper, the *Neue Freie Presse*, called Hermann Ungar 'the most important writer of the decade'. And that in one of the most hectic decades in German literature when, among the younger generation, figures such as Franz Werfel, Joseph Roth, Ernst Toller, Alfred Döblin, Bertolt Brecht, Leo Perutz, Paul Kornfeld, Ernst Weiss, Egon Erwin Kisch were active. Unlike another German-speaking Jewish writer from the region that was to become Czechoslovakia, Franz Kafka, with whom his name is often linked, Ungar was almost completely forgotten in Germany after the Second World War. In France, however, the issue of translations of his two novels and a volume with two short stories in 1987–88 (the stories and *The Maimed* had already appeared in France in the 1920s) was greeted with enthusiastic reviews and the recognition not only of his importance in the context of German literature between the wars, but of the abiding power of his portrayal of a world in which all the figures seem to be cripples: physical, psychological, emotional and moral cripples.

One critic, Vincent Ostria, declared that the excesses of punk musicians such as Sid Vicious looked 'small beer' compared to the extremes possible in literature as demonstrated by Ungar's novels. Both French and German critics have insisted on seeing in his characters, in which full humanity has been reduced to fear and hatred – often the hatred of their own selves – an adumbration of figures which in 1933 would 'step out of literary fiction and into reality'.

Hermann Ungar was born in 1893 in the Moravian town of Boskovice, into a wealthy, cultured Jewish family. His father owned a distillery and was mayor of the Jewish community, whose presence in the town went back to the 11th century. Boskovice was entirely Czech-speaking, but the Jewish community – until the end of the First World War the two parts of the town were separate – spoke German. Ungar grew up speaking both languages, but his education at both high school and university was at German institutions.

The routine anti-semitism of some of his German fellow pupils in the high school in Brno awakened an interest in Judaism and the Jewish religion, to which he had been largely indifferent until then. He decided to study Hebrew and Arabic in Berlin and joined the Jewish student corporation modelled on the German duelling fraternities, acting as its president in 1914, although by then he had transferred from Semitic languages to Law.

As with many other artists and writers, the war was an experience which fundamentally changed his outlook. He volunteered in 1914 and served for three years in the artillery before being seriously wounded and invalided out. He resumed his studies, completing his law degree at the (German) University of Prague in 1918. But this was a different Ungar. He abandoned the student fraternities, with their duels and colours, and renounced Zionism, which seemed to him in danger of becoming a new kind of nationalism.

He also seems to have thrown away or destroyed all his early writings, plays full of passion, violence and intrigue. It had always been Ungar's ambition to be a writer and for a short while he worked in the theatre in Eger/Egra, hoping it would be a milieu conducive to writing, but after a short time took a position in a bank. This led to work for the Czech Export Agency in Berlin and finally, in 1922, a post as commercial attaché at the Czech embassy there. Though the work was not particularly congenial to him, the Czech foreign ministry treated him generously, apparently pleased to encourage a man making a name for himself in German literature. (A press attaché at the embassy was another Czech-German writer, Camill Hoffmann.) In 1928 he was moved to the foreign ministry in Prague; on 10 October 1929 he resigned from his post; on 15 October his second son was born; on 28 October he died of peritonitis.

The works he wrote around the end of the war did not reach the public: a novel has disappeared and a play called *Krieg* (War) was not published until 1990. Two stories, gathered together under the title *Knaben und Mörder* (Boys and Murderers) appeared in 1920. *The Maimed* was published in 1923, to a reaction of horrified admiration, and his second novel, *Die Klasse*, in 1927. In 1928 his play *Der rote General* (The Red General) was performed with great success in Berlin. The central figure is a Jewish general who is abandoned by the Communists, once he is no longer needed, and executed by the White Russians. Some saw it as a portrait of Trotsky, which Ungar denied. A second play, a comedy called *Die Gartenlaube* (The Arbour), had its premiere six weeks after his death.

There is something of a Jekyll-and-Hyde about Ungar. He was known as an elegant, charming, witty and sociable diplomat while his writings display the opposite qualities, showing the world as a bleak place where love is at best lust and mostly turns to hatred, often ending in bloody violence. The heroes of his two novels try to avoid this by doing as little as possible, fearing the slightest self-assertion might set the chaos in motion that they feel is constantly threatening. They try, unsuccessfully, to cocoon themselves in arid routine, so that even before they are dragged down to destruction their lives are empty of any real fulfilment.

The powerful impact of Ungar's two novels is in part due to the extreme economy of his style. Everything is narrated in a plain, sober, detached manner, without authorial comment, or even evidence of an authorial attitude. His themes recall those of Expressionism, his style is closer to that of the 'New Objectivity' of the mid-to-late 1920s.

Ungar makes use of psychological and social factors. In *The Maimed*, Polzer's feelings of guilt and revulsion towards women are 'explained' by incidents during his childhood (the one point where an authorial voice speaks directly to the reader), and his insecurity and inhibitions by the shame he feels at his humble social origins. But the purpose of the novel is not the illustration of social themes or psychological types. Ungar uses these factors to set up the central characters, but, despite the sobriety of the narration, the aim is not realism.

As in Kafka's stories, the reader experiences Ungar's fiction at an existential level. They give us a feeling of the way life is, not of what a particular society is like, or how a particular type of person behaves. What makes them more pessimistic than Kafka is the lack of any transcendental dimension, even an empty or unattainable one. There is no sense that these fictions are parables. To use a current phrase, 'what you see is what you get'.

This can be confirmed by looking at the religious motifs in *The Maimed*. Polzer has a picture of St. Francis over his bed, which gives him a sense of security. But it is not the thought of the *saint* the picture represents that comforts him, but the familiar *object*. His attachment to the picture of St. Francis is an object-oriented fetishism, similar to his mania for counting his possessions.

What makes Ungar's world so irredeemably bleak is ultimately this lack of any spiritual dimension. It is a powerful, almost mesmerising portrayal; there appears to be no way out once you are inside it. This, too, distinguishes it from Kafka and is perhaps one reason why Ungar has not enjoyed even a modicum of the same kind of posthumous success. One cannot imagine his novels spawning the multitudinous interpretations of, for example, *The Trial*. It is precisely the uncompromising nature of the vision they present which makes them stand out from the writings of his contemporaries and which, if there were justice in such matters, would guarantee them a lasting place in the history of 20th-century literature.

From the age of twenty-four onward Franz Polzer was employed in a bank. Every morning he set off for his office at a quarter to eight, never a minute earlier or later. When he came out of the side-street in which he lived, the tower clock struck three times.

During all the time he worked for the bank Franz Polzer had changed neither his position there, nor his lodgings. He had moved into them when he abandoned his course at university and started work. His landlady was a widow of roughly his own age. At the time he took the room with her, she was still in mourning for her late husband.

In all the years he was employed by the bank, Franz Polzer was never out in the streets during the morning, apart from on Sundays. The mornings of working-days, when the shops were open and people in a hurry jostled each other in the streets, were unknown to him. He had never been absent from the bank for a single day.

The streets through which he passed presented the same scene every morning. The blinds of the shops were being raised. Clerks were standing by the doors, waiting for their bosses. Every day he met the same people, schoolboys and schoolgirls, faded secretaries and sullen men hurrying to their offices. He made his way among these people who shared his morning hour, was one of them, hurrying, unnoticing and unnoticed.

Franz Polzer had been told that, given his abilities, he could, with industry and application, rise to a senior position in his profession. Through all the years he had never reflected on the fact that the hopes he pinned on his career had not been fulfilled. He had forgotten them. He forgot them in all the little activities into which, from the very beginning, his time had been divided up. He got out of bed in the morning, washed, dressed, glanced at the news-paper while he was having his breakfast, and went to the bank. He sat down at his desk, on which were piles of papers which he had to compare with entries in the ledgers on the shelves all round him. He signed each sheet, when he had checked it, with the initials of his name and placed it in a file. All around the office, and in the other rooms, there were many other men and women sitting, like him, at desks that looked just the same as his. The whole building was filled with the smell of these men and women, with the noise of their monotonous activity and conversa-tions. Franz Polzer was equal to the demands his work made on him. It offered no opportunity of dis-tinguishing himself and therefore no chance of attracting the attention of his superiors.

He took his midday meal in a small inn close to the bank. The afternoons passed in the same way as the mornings. At six o'clock he tidied up the papers and pencils on his desk, locked his drawer and went home. The widow brought a simple supper to his room. He took off his shoes, jacket and shirt-collar. After his supper he spent an hour reading the news-paper from end to end. Then he went to bed. His sleep was restless, but he seldom had dreams. When he did dream, he dreamed that he had forgotten his initials, which he had to write hundreds of times a day, that his hand was paralysed or that his pencil wouldn't write.

In the morning Franz Polzer got up as on every other morning before and began his day, which passed like all the other days. He was sullen and morose, but he never became conscious of the fact that there could be something other than spending every day sitting at his desk in the bank, that you could get up later, stroll round the streets, eat two soft-boiled eggs for breakfast in a café and take lunch in a good restaurant.

There was one interruption to this monotonous routine which Franz Polzer remembered particularly. The death of his father.

Franz Polzer had never been close to his father. Part of the reason was probably the fact that his mother had died when he was very young. Perhaps she would have been able to reduce the friction between them. His father was a small shopkeeper in a little country town. Polzer's room was next to his father's shop. His father was a harsh, hard-working and unapproachable man. From his earliest childhood Franz Polzer had to help out in his father's shop, so that he had hardly enough time left to do his homework. Despite that, his father demanded good school reports from his son. Once, when Polzer had a poor mark, his father made him go without his supper for four weeks. Polzer was seventeen at the time.

A sister of his father's lived with them, a widow without children who had moved in after the death of Polzer's mother to keep house for his father. Polzer had the vague notion that his father's sister had forced his dead mother out of the house and from the very first made no attempt to conceal his dislike of her. His aunt made no secret of her feelings either. She called him a bad boy who would never get anywhere in life, called him greedy and lazy. She gave him so little to eat, he was forced to make himself a copy of the key to her cupboard and steal things secretly at night in his father's house.

On top of all this came an incident which can only be described with the strongest reservations. At the time Polzer was fourteen and had the easily aroused imagination of adolescent boys, stimulated, moreover, by hatred. He could only imagine the relationship between the sexes as something horrible, something fundamentally disgusting. The very idea of the body of a naked woman filled him with loathing. He had once gone into his aunt's room while she was washing, stripped to the waist. The sight of her withered body, of her tired, drooping flesh etched itself on his mind and remained lodged in his memory. Once, during the night, he was standing by the open bread cupboard in the darkened hall behind the shop when the door of his aunt's room opened. He pressed himself against the wall. Out of the bright doorway came his father in his nightshirt. For a brief moment, like a shadow, the image of his sister appeared behind him. His aunt bolted the door from inside.

His father passed close by him. His nightshirt was open and Polzer thought he could see his hairy chest, despite the darkness. For a moment he caught the smell of fresh rolls that always hung about his father, presumably from the shop. Polzer held his breath and was still frozen to the spot long after the bedroom door had closed behind his father.

This experience made an impression on Franz Polzer which was to have the most lasting effect on his later life. Despite the fact that he had only seen his aunt's shadow, he firmly believed that at that moment his aunt had been naked. From that point on he was tormented by images of the wild scenes that must be taking place at night between his father and his father's sister. Polzer had no other evidence, apart from that one nocturnal episode. Nor did anything happen subsequently to give substance to his belief.

Now Polzer's nights were sleepless until day began to break. He listened. He thought he could hear doors creaking and cautious, hesitant footsteps on the rotten floorboards of the old house. He would start out of a light sleep, sure he had heard a suppressed cry. He was filled with bitter disgust. At the same time his curiosity impelled him to creep up to his aunt's door at night. He never heard anything other than the sound of her breathing.

His father often beat Franz Polzer while his aunt held him, and he dreamed of his father, horrified beyond measure in his dream at the way he looked, at his dirty clothes, his dull, red dream-face, with his aunt standing behind, encouraging his father to beat and torment him. After such nights, during the day

19

when he was bound to cross his father's path, he wanted to be beaten by him again. It was as if he were compelled to make everything reality, including his hatred of his father, by having the latter hit him on the back with his heavy fists. Yet he felt he was grown up, was conscious of the fact, only he was weaker, much weaker than his father.

Some people who lived on the first floor had a maid called Milka. She wore a loose blouse and often came into the shop. Once Polzer saw his father feel her breasts. That evening Polzer dropped a plate on the floor. His father beat him and his aunt dug her fingers into his skinny flesh. He didn't cry, which made his father beat him all the more furiously, and that was what Franz Polzer wanted.

Whenever he could, he escaped from the shop and hung around the streets of the little town, simply so as not to have to be at home. He often spent the whole day in the house of a rich man called Fanta, whose son went to the high school with him. There was a close friendship between Polzer and Karl Fanta. At first Polzer had only entered the Fantas' house with the greatest reluctance. He knew that the Jews had murdered the Saviour and that they served their God with dark and cruel rites. He was convinced that it would not only be a grave sin for a Roman Catholic, but also a great danger to visit a Jew's house regularly. Milka had worked for a Jewish family. She told his aunt in the shop about it. She had run away before Easter. She had been afraid. It was only gradually that Polzer overcame his qualms through his love for Karl Fanta. Karl Fanta saw that

Polzer felt unhappy and the two boys often embraced and kissed amid tears.

Polzer did not dare pour out his heart to Karl Fanta. He had grown up in the small, cramped house, in the grubby shop where he spent his free time among sacks of flour and pepper, barrels of pickled gherkins and tins of sweets, asking humble folk what they wanted or sweeping the floor. He was ashamed of the shop. He was ashamed of his father, whose jacket always had a dusting of flour, who stepped respectfully to one side whenever a rich inhabitant walked past, of his aunt, who went out without a hat and whose hair was greying at the temples and tousled by the wind. She did not tie it up in a headscarf, the white line of her parting was always visible between the black hair on either side. His friend's mother was a tall, elegant lady who wore jewellery and dark clothes. She had pale, finely chiselled features like her son, who resembled her very closely. She too had black hair like his aunt, but hers was combed into a chignon. Both she and her son had a shimmer of tiny bluish veins at the temples. The most beautiful thing about both her and her son were their slim, white hands. Karl's father was a stout gentleman who spoke in calm, measured tones, self-assured and dignified. In this milieu, in the presence of his handsome friend, Polzer found it impossible to talk about his father's little corner grocery store.

Polzer brushed his suit and used books to press his trousers. He wanted to look like a schoolboy from a good middle-class home and not like the son of a small shopkeeper. He kept his hands, which were rough and red from working in the shop, hidden from people, a habit which made him seem very awkward and unsure of himself and which he never overcame, even later in life. If a stranger was visiting Karl's parents and quietly asked his host about Franz Polzer, the latter felt himself flush with embarrassment. Even if the question was put so quietly, so unobtrusively that Franz Polzer did not hear it, he still sensed it with his immensely acute inward ear.

All he wanted was to come from a 'good' family. Years later he still blushed when questioned about his background and gave evasive answers. Sometimes he would lie and say his father had been a high-school teacher or a judge. Once he even claimed to be the son of a factory owner. Immediately he felt his questioner run an appraising eye over his suit and was painfully aware of the shabbiness of his appearance.

It was Karl Fanta's father who made it possible for him to go to the university in the capital. Polzer started together with Karl. He studied medicine, Karl law. Polzer was glad to get away from home, no longer to be constantly confronted with the shame of the shop, no longer to have to submit to his father's strict discipline, to see the parting in his aunt's hair and endure her scolding. There was only one memory he took with him from home, one that had been dear above all things to him. The memory of his mother. He had scarcely known her. He believed he remembered her having him brought to her death-bed, where she lay with her hair spread over the pillow. She pressed him to her and his hair was damp with her tears. This memory always warmed his heart. His love for his mother was a refuge from his hatred of his aunt. The stronger his dislike of her became, the more that love had grown.

Polzer's relationship with Karl was as close as possible between young people of the same age. Polzer was happy for the opportunity to live his life at the side of this handsome young man whose impervious self-assurance he admired no less than the classical proportions of his physique. Karl always behaved in a friendly way towards him and it was Polzer's desire to anticipate Karl's every wish and to perform little services for him. He laid out his underlinen and made sure Karl's clothes were spotless. Karl had black hair that felt like silk. Despite his open and friendly manner, Polzer often felt that inwardly Karl was ignoring him. He longed for some small token of affection, a repetition of those boyhood kisses. It was a yearning that remained unfulfilled.

At the university Polzer was praised for his industry and his intelligence. He passed his preliminary examinations with distinction. Then Karl fell ill and the doctors sent him to the south, where he was to remain for a year. No longer a paid companion to his rich friend, it was impossible for Polzer to continue at the university and he had to be thankful that Karl's father found him a position in the bank.

After a short time at the bank he was a changed man. In the face of his work, everything else melted away. Punctuality, routine, the inescapable certainty of what the next day would bring all destroyed him. His life was completely absorbed by activities that divided up his time. During those seventeen years he hardly ever went out and met people. Thus he became unsure of himself whenever he had to do something different from what he was in the habit of doing. If he had to talk to a stranger, he suddenly couldn't find the words he needed. He always had the feeling that his clothes were inappropriate, didn't fit him and made him look ridiculous. The least departure from routine confused him. He insisted everything be kept meticulously in its habitual place. Every day the newspaper had to be placed on exactly the same spot on the table, parallel to the edge. His pedantry went so far that it irritated him if the cords of the blinds did not hang straight and did not form a right angle where they met the window-ledge. Annoyed, he would go and adjust them.

Franz Polzer had been at the bank for about ten years when his father died. The funeral fell on a Sunday, so that he did not have to miss a day's work. On the Saturday afternoon he left the city by train.

Polzer retained lasting and most unpleasant memories of the day of the funeral. On the journey there he could not find a seat on the crowded train and so had to stand all the way. His feet, unused to such exertion, were sore for days afterwards. He arrived in a bad mood to a sullen welcome from his aunt, who probably thought he had come to claim his father's shop. Despite the bitter winter cold, the bedroom waiting for him was unheated, and his sleep in his old bed was tormented by bad dreams. In the morning he found no breakfast had been prepared for him. He felt it would be wrong to go to an inn and so had to attend the funeral on an empty stomach. People whom he scarcely knew came up and shook his hand. His aunt stood beside his father's laid-out corpse in the middle of the room, Polzer in a dark corner, like a stranger.

When the priest began the benediction, Polzer had to go and stand beside his aunt. Only now did he see his father. He was wearing a black jacket that had creases across the chest. His hair had gone quite grey. His face looked small and hollow-cheeked. The sight of the corpse had no effect whatsoever on Polzer. His response to it was no different than to any extraneous object. He did not feel reminded of his father. At the cemetery his aunt took his arm and wept noisily. Polzer stood in the slushy snow and felt the damp seeping in through his shoes. He knew how susceptible to colds he was and restlessly kept changing feet.

Everyone's eyes were on Franz Polzer, observing and scrutinising him. The attention he attracted disconcerted him. In his discomfiture he several times felt the buttons of his flies, repeatedly assuring himself that they were fastened. This conspicuous gesture caused him great embarrassment but still did not stop the feeling of nakedness forcing him to repeat it a few minutes later.

After the funeral was over Franz Polzer told his aunt that he did not want to inherit anything from his father's estate. His father had not left any money. The mortgage on the house had not been paid off. Polzer did not want any clothes or pieces of furniture. He wanted no memento.

The widow was pale and thin when Polzer moved into her house as her lodger after Karl Fanta had left for the south. The mourning dress hung loosely about her body. It was in the first months after her husband's death. Her skin was yellowish, like old paper. Only later did her figure fill out, her hips broaden.

She was called Klara Porges. Afterwards it seemed to Polzer as if her name had been the cause of everything. From the very first the name had annoyed him. The combination appeared both incredibly ridiculous and irritating at the same time.

Polzer lived alone with Frau Porges. One of the rooms was empty. The chairs in that room were draped in linen dust-covers. Frau Porges had to do all the housework herself, for there was no maid. But Polzer cleaned his own shoes. The widow wanted to take on that chore as well, but he would not let her. He had always attached great importance to polishing his shoes himself and he had never come across anyone whose shoes shone like his. To a brief glance they looked like patent-leather shoes. At home he had had to polish his father's and his aunt's shoes, but he had not taken great pains with them. He devoted half an hour every morning to cleaning his shoes. He used several brushes and cloths of varying fineness one after the other. Frau Porges expressed the opinion that it was a task unsuited to a man.

Polzer, however, knew how pleasant, how refreshing it was to go out in the morning with properly polished shoes on your feet. He pointed out that there was nothing unmanly at all about this occupation, reminding Frau Porges that everywhere where they had manservants, in hotels or rich people's houses for example, the task was performed by men.

From the very first the widow surrounded him with care and attention. He let her deal with everything he found disturbing. That was above all any out-of-the-ordinary events that might occur. The least departure from routine filled him with anxiety and consternation. The knowledge that on one of the next days he would have to go into a shop to buy something made him uneasy. Immediately he felt as if he had no time for anything else, as if he had no room for anything else in his whole life. His thoughts constantly revolved round it, the fear of forgetting tormented him. He worked out the amount of time necessary and prepared what he would say. Things might crop up that could not be foreseen. In particular, the price demanded might be greater than the sum he had with him. Payments, such as the rent, which were due on specific days, kept him awake for weeks beforehand. He would spend the nights counting the money. During the day, when his mind was on other things, or at night while he was asleep, he would suddenly start at the realisation that at that particular moment he had forgotten about it, and he reproached himself for being able to forget something he should not. But Frau Porges was prepared to take his salary at the beginning of every month and see to everything herself. She gave Polzer a few crowns each week to pay for his lunch at the office and his tram ticket. Now she even purchased new articles of clothing for him, so that he did not have to go into the shop, or even know anything about it.

This all happened despite the fact that Polzer's attitude to Frau Porges remained distant. He was alarmed by the tender, motherly looks in which she tried to ensnare him. There was something uncomfortable about them, a desire to come closer, a closeness. Polzer did not see her very much, only when she brought his breakfast in the mornings and his supper in the evenings. He avoided her eyes and refused to get into conversation with her. He lived in the next room to the widow, he could hear her breathing at night, could hear her bed creak when she turned over in her sleep. But in all the years, he had never been together with her in the same room for more than a few minutes.

From the very first, the presence of Frau Porges had filled him with disquiet. Her hair gave off a smell that reminded him vaguely of soap. She had a parting down the middle, like his aunt. On top of that, whenever he saw her, he didn't know why, but an image of her naked body immediately appeared unbidden in his mind. It filled him with a deep sense of shame and disgust. It was the image of a shadowy black body. This image became more and more obsessive, the more her figure filled out.

Since the earliest days of his youth such images had filled him with revulsion. In the years before he took the room with Frau Porges, Polzer would not

have gone with women if Karl, who did not understand his revulsion, had not taken him and forced
him to have intercourse with them. Polzer often
threw up after he left the brothel where Karl had
taken him. Even as a boy the sight of women had
filled him with alarm. He avoided Milka because he
could sense, beneath the loose blouse which drew his
eye, the constantly changing shape of her round
breasts. He did not dare look at Milka's breasts.
When Karl told him that the older lads used to go to
the woods to meet Milka, he avoided touching
Milka's hands when he was alone in the shop and had
to take a coin from her. Milka's hands filled him with
horror. Milka must have noticed that he kept out of
her way and she often tried to grab him and pull him
to her. Once she came across him on the dark staircase. He pressed himself against the wall in an alcove
where the Saviour hung on a wooden cross. She came
up to him and laughed, she could see that he was
afraid. Her hands grasped him. He did not move. She
fumbled with his buttons. He trembled. She took
hold of his penis. Milka laughed when his sperm
came and gave him a shove that sent him staggering.

When the shadow of his aunt had appeared in the
light of the open doorway, Franz Polzer already
knew how terrible a woman's nakedness was. At the
shadow of his aunt, as at the sight of Frau Porges, he
was tormented by the terrible thought that this
naked body was not closed up. That a ghastly slit
yawned on bottomless depths. Like flesh cut open,
like the folds of skin along a gaping wound. He
refused to look at the pictures and statues of naked

29

women in art galleries. He did not want ever to touch the body of a naked woman. It seemed to him there must be uncleanness there and a disgusting smell. He only saw Frau Porges during the day, in her clothes. In spite of that, he was tormented by the image of her fat, naked body.

When Frau Porges came into his room, Polzer kept his eyes on the newspaper and avoided looking at her. Despite that, he noticed how her figure became more rounded year by year. Sometimes he could feel her eyes on him. At such moments he did not dare move. He never understood how it had come to that first conversation between them. He had thought she scarcely paid any attention to him either. It happened one evening when she brought him his supper. Everything started with that evening.

Polzer was sitting at the table when she came in. He fixed his eyes on the newspaper, although he wasn't reading. Uneasily, he waited for the door to close behind her. He heard her steps go towards the door. Suddenly he knew that she was standing by the door, looking at him. He kept his eyes glued to the paper. He could feel she wanted him to say something, but he said nothing. He was going to wait and not move until she left.

Then he heard her sob. He looked up. She put her face in her hands and started to weep bitter tears.

It worried him that while she was crying she lost her breath and had to gasp for air. He realised he had to do something and stood up. He had no idea what to do. Completely at a loss, he asked her to calm down and tell him the reason for her sorrow. But

Frau Porges did not calm down. She had sunk to the ground and was gasping for breath in a manner that was becoming more and more alarming. So Polzer went over to her and tried to pull her hands away from her face. At the same time he helped her to her feet.

She stopped crying and began to speak, haltingly at first, interrupted by sobs. The cause of her distress, she said, was his heartless behaviour towards her, a poor, abandoned widow. She worked her fingers to the bone looking after him and in all the years she had not heard one little word of thanks from him.

Polzer had moved away from her and did not interrupt.

'You treat me like a servant,' she said.

She was silent and seemed to be expecting an answer.

'I wouldn't dream of it, Frau Porges,' he replied.

'You do,' she said. 'Like a servant. You never ask me what I do when I've finished my work, how I'm going to spend my Sunday. You go out, and I'm left alone in the apartment.'

'I omitted to do so, Frau Porges, because it never occurred to me, and because I did not know you valued my company. But if you wish, we can go for a walk together on Sunday, Frau Porges.'

She gave Polzer a joyful look. He suddenly realised with horror what he had said.

'We'll go out to Kuchelbad,' she said. 'First thing in the morning.'

'In the afternoon, Frau Porges,' replied Polzer.

*

31

That happened on Thursday. He spent Friday and
Saturday in a sweat of agitation. He heard Frau
Porges singing as she busied herself with the pots
and pans in the kitchen. He passed her on the stairs.
She looked at him with a meaningful smile. Polzer
decided to flee.

That was during the Saturday night. He checked
his things and thought out a plan. He had to leave
the building in the morning, while she was still
asleep. He had to find somewhere to live in one of the
districts outside the city centre. He had seen room-
to-let signs on houses. He resolved to be cautious and
enquire whether there were young women or children
there before he took the room. Also to observe the
people to see if they looked honest. There were
increasing reports of thefts, of murders even.

Towards morning it suddenly occurred to him that
it would mean losing all his belongings and that he
had no money because Frau Porges looked after it.
Moreover she could always wait for him outside the
bank. He realised there was no escape from her.

Besides the revulsion, with which the prospect of
being together with Frau Porges for several hours
filled him, he was troubled by the break with routine
which this event represented. Franz Polzer was in the
habit of taking a particular walk on Sunday afternoon. He left the apartment at four o-clock, crossed
Charles Square and headed for the Embankment,
where he walked along the river for a short distance.
At particular spots he would stop and look at the
river. Then he turned off towards the city centre.

At five o'clock he went into a small café and sat

down at a table in the billiard-room. He watched the billiard players. Watching them put him in an exalted mood. He followed the smooth balls as they rolled across the green cloth and enjoyed the clear, bright click when they collided. At the same time he observed the movements of the players as they leant forward over the table, preparing for their shot. He meticulously counted the points each player scored. His great desire was to see one of them score an endless series of cannons, he held his breath at every shot and was disappointed and hurt whenever it missed.

He longed to play billiards himself, but it was a longing that was never to be fulfilled. He shrank from the idea of putting his body movements on public display. Once, later on, the doctor asked him to play. Polzer already had the cue in his hand, aware that he had to chalk the tip carefully. Then he remembered he had held a cue in his hand once before. He had the feeling there had been people there. At the moment he could not say whether it had been a dream or not. But it couldn't really have been anything else. When he had started to chalk the cue, it had grown and become heavy, and he had lost his balance.

With a shudder, Polzer remembered this and carefully placed the cue back in the stand.

Towards dawn Polzer wondered whether to pretend to be ill. He rejected the idea, as he had never had one day's illness since he had been living at Frau Porges's. There was no other way of getting out of it. If heavy rain should make the outing impossible, it was to be feared that Frau Porges would go with him to a café. Surely that would be more embarrassing than the excursion.

Polzer had no idea how Frau Porges dressed to go out. He had never met her outside the apartment. Perhaps, like his aunt, she had no hat. He didn't dare ask. He certainly couldn't count on her being elegant. But even if she came without a hat, he was going to have to appear beside her in public.

Since Kuchelbad was a popular place for an outing, a great crush of people was to be expected. Polzer imagined how he would have to push his way to the booking office for tickets and stand squashed in among strangers on the small boat, if, that is, he was quick enough to be one of those at the front who got on board. He had sometimes watched the panic of such moments from the Embankment. Also, the pushing and shoving as people got onto the steamboat provided an ideal opportunity for pickpockets. Polzer decided to leave his pocket watch at home.

On the Sunday morning he had hardly put his fork down when Frau Porges came in. She was well dressed. She was wearing a black suit with a long jacket, a little black hat with a veil, black gloves and was carrying a leather handbag and an umbrella. Polzer put on his jacket. He stuffed the newspaper into his coat pocket.

The landing stage was full of people. From the list of fares Polzer saw that second-class tickets were not too dear and decided to travel second class. He had always liked travelling in comfort. Frau Porges saw to it that they got two seats. She immediately started talking far too loud. Polzer checked to make sure there was no one he knew on board. He gave no answer to Frau Porges, since he was disturbed by the feeling that those around might follow their conversation. At that Frau Porges fell silent.

In Kuchelbad, Polzer and Frau Porges climbed a hill where there were hardly any people. It occurred to Polzer that, should he feel a call of nature, he would not have the opportunity of getting away from Frau Porges for a few moments. Shortly after that, he began to feel signs that filled him with unease. His anxiety grew when there was no doubt about his need. He could see no way of explaining why he had to disappear into the bushes, despite the fact that the agonising urge was developing into excruciatingly painful pressure.

He spread out his overcoat on the hillside. They sat next to each other. He took the newspaper out of the pocket and started to read. Half-jokingly, Frau Porges told him off. The setting sun was shining on her face. He noticed that her cheeks were covered with downy hairs.

'You don't want to talk to me at all,' said Frau Porges, with a sigh. 'You take me on an excursion and then stare into space, not saying a word. I was so looking forward to it and now you've made me quite sad.'

'That was not my intention, Frau Porges,' said Polzer.

'Really? That wasn't your intention? You didn't want to spoil my enjoyment?'

Frau Porges moved a little closer to him.

'No, that was not my intention, Frau Porges,' he said, without looking at her.

'I think you're quite different from the way you seem. I'm right there, aren't I?'

'That is not for me to say, Frau Porges. But let us assume so, Frau Porges, let us assume so.'

' "Frau Porges" all the time, "Frau Porges"! When we've been together for so long! No one would believe it, even if you told them.' She looked at him tenderly. 'Call me Frau Klara.'

'No,' replied Polzer at once.

It was evening by the time they were back on the boat. Sitting down, Polzer's pain became even more excruciating. He noticed a senior official from the Accounts Department close by. The boat was packed. It sank down to one side, then pitched and tossed. Frau Porges gave a little shriek and clung onto his arm. It was completely dark.

'Let go of me at once,' he said.

He pressed his thighs together. He thought his bladder was about to burst.

'What's the matter with you?' asked Frau Porges.

'Something dreadful,' he said, in an expressionless voice, 'something dreadful.'

When they were back on land, Polzer could hardly walk. Frau Porges took his arm and supported him. Polzer did not resist.

He ground his teeth in pain and moaned softly. With every step he was afraid his will-power would finally give way to the urge. They were walking down a dimly lit side-street. Frau Porges stopped. She looked all round.

'Now,' she said, 'that's enough. No one can see you.'

Polzer could not have put up with it any longer. He just managed to undo his buttons in time. Then he released himself from the tormenting pain.

It was only when he heard the noise that he realised what he was doing. It seemed inordinately loud and he tried in vain to reduce the sound.

At Charles Square they passed the lighted windows of a café.

'We'll go and have a coffee,' said Frau Porges.

He didn't dare say no. They went in and sat down at a small window table. There was no one he knew in the café.

Polzer was ashamed of the weakness which had humiliated him in front of Frau Porges. She was looking at him and he realised he had to say something, despite the embarrassing nature of the whole matter. He felt that she expected it.

'Frau Porges,' he began, 'you have the right to demand an explanation. I must admit that for a brief while I forgot the fact that you are a lady, something to which your suggestion may well have contributed, Frau Porges. I think I would be right in saying I would never have done it of my own accord.'

'You show great consideration,' said Frau Porges. 'I'm delighted you treat me as a lady, even though I'm just a simple woman who hasn't even got a maid.'

He felt she had not quite understood him. He

realised how discourteous his general behaviour towards Frau Porges had been. For a moment he considered addressing her as 'madam' from now on, but dropped the idea because he did not know how to explain such a change to her.

On the dark stairs Frau Porges was overcome with fear and pressed up against Polzer. He had no matches on him and spoke a few calming words.

As they said good night, Frau Porges indicated how much she was looking forward to next Sunday. For the moment Polzer avoided saying anything in reply.

A picture of Polzer's patron saint hung over his bed. It was not much bigger than a postcard, white and square. In the middle was the saint, painted in bright colours. The picture was framed and under glass.

The picture came from Polzer's mother. At one time the saint had hung in his mother's room among other brightly coloured pictures of saints. Polzer's mother had been devout. Every day she poured oil into the lamp that hung at the feet of the Saviour on the dark staircase and burnt with a flickering light at night. She also used to take him with her to church. Franz Polzer could remember those early times in church well. He used to kneel beside his mother beneath the big, dark pictures, plagued with fearful thoughts. He was afraid of the bleeding figures of the martyrs yet still could not take his eyes off them. They were half-naked, their bodies were painted red, their faces contorted with suffering and turned upwards. Polzer would leave the church oppressed by images of sin and torment, and fearful that he might have somehow committed sacrilege. He only stopped attending church regularly when he moved in with Karl Fanta. From then on he only went to church rarely and in secret.

The picture also hung over his bed during the time he lived with Karl. He had a special relationship with the picture of St. Francis. He would never have slept for one single night without the protection of the picture over his bed and he took it with him even on short journeys. He had the feeling that in some mysterious way the fate of the picture was tied to his own. Despite that, he never had the idea of a personal saint protecting him. He thought of the picture, never of the patron saint it represented.

During the night, the picture hung over his bed. Polzer never slept well. At night he lay awake and heard creaking noises. He thought there were shuffling footsteps approaching and he was afraid. Despite the fact that it only increased his agitation, in the evenings he read reports of murders and trials in the newspaper. He cut these articles out of the paper, dated them and kept them in a folder in his desk.

Also in the evenings he often read books which Frau Porges borrowed from a library. They contained descriptions of crimes and the adventures of detectives. He read all these things out of a vague desire to prove that his nocturnal fears were justified. Danger was present, of that there was no doubt. There was one thought that calmed him during those nights, the thought of the picture over his bed. He never asked himself whether it might be capable of protecting him. Its very presence calmed him. As if it confirmed that everything was in order, everything was in its place, that even in the incalculable darkness nothing had changed and that he himself had done nothing that might breach the solid order of routine and thus open the way to something out of the ordinary.

While he was living with Karl, the picture drew down Karl's mockery on Polzer. Karl called him superstitious. It never occurred to him that Polzer's relationship to the picture could be a relationship to order, that superstition could be a punctilious attention to order and routine or fear of the danger presented by something out of the ordinary. For decades Polzer had used a penholder which he had bought while he was still at school. It was a simple, black, folding penholder. While he was at school he would not have dared do his homework with any other pen. At university and in the bank he still wrote with that pen, which he always carried with him. Suddenly the black penholder had disappeared. It happened at the time when the widow made her first advances, and Polzer was in no doubt that Frau Porges must have hidden the penholder because she knew the state of agitation in which the disappearance of this old pen would be sure to leave him.

Polzer could not bring himself voluntarily to part with things that belonged to him. Old documents, newspapers, cast-off articles of clothing all piled up in his cupboards and drawers. The terrible thought of burglaries haunted him constantly. He was perpetually worried that items in his possession might be lost without his realising. Polzer could find no way of overcoming the permanent feeling of unease this tormenting thought caused him. All his senses had to be unceasingly on the alert, for the danger was there. No change must escape his notice. Once a week he counted his belongings: books, newspapers, documents, linen, clothes. He wanted to be sure there had been no change in the tally of his possessions.

Polzer knew he possessed no great treasures. He

was in no doubt that his meagre belongings, his repeatedly mended underwear, his threadbare suits, were of no value and scarcely likely to tempt someone to steal them. Nevertheless he could not shake off that fear. It took hold of him the moment darkness fell. Night harboured all manner of dangers. He was defenceless and he did not trust the solitude around him. Something was hiding, the darkness breathed conspiracy and Polzer could do nothing about it. The plot against him creaked, breathed and lurked at the door. Once the first stone was loosened, it could make a breach, pour in and gain a foothold. Polzer's belongings were counted, the cords of the blinds formed right angles, order had not yet been disturbed. The picture hung over the bed in witness.

Franz Polzer longed for someone to share his room, someone whose tangible presence would have silenced the sound of the hostile solitude. He longed to have someone sleeping beside him. He heard Frau Porges's bed creak under the burden of her body and resolved to ask her in the morning to let him sleep in her room. He would buy a folding screen to put between their beds. He wanted to come through the night refreshed and rested like her. In the morning he rejected the idea. Her meaningful looks put him off. He was afraid she would not understand the genuine reason for his request. It seemed not unlikely that she would take the opportunity to come over to him and embrace him, as she always seemed ready to do. The likelihood of that happening discouraged him. He straightened up, when the widow came in, and threw out his chest. At the same time he let his arms hang down loosely and pushed his head as far back as possible. That was his wordless resistance.

On Polzer's desk was a box of writing paper.

There was no one he corresponded with and it was rare that he had to write a letter. But he believed it was necessary to be prepared for that eventuality. In the morning after a sleepless night he often felt the need to count the sheets of writing paper. The knowledge that none was missing calmed him.

Once Frau Porges came in while he was counting the sheets of paper. She was bringing his breakfast. She looked at Polzer, not saying a word. He felt he had been caught in a shameful act. At the same time he was annoyed that she had started coming in without knocking.

'You didn't knock, Frau Porges,' he said.

He felt it only made his situation worse.

'Herr Polzer,' said Frau Porges, 'I've known this for a long time. You're trying to insult me. Nothing like this has ever happened to me before. It will be best if we go our separate ways.'

She was angry with him and came closer. He retreated towards the window.

'You know very well,' she said, 'that no one comes into this room apart from me. You think I'm stealing! I'll have to find a lodger who trusts me.'

'Frau Porges!' said Franz Polzer, very alarmed. 'You can't mean that, Frau Porges. If knocking at the door is too much trouble, then don't knock, Frau Porges. Come in without knocking! But throw me out of your apartment? No, Frau Porges, you can't do that. You know that the cupboards are full of my things. I don't know what is where any more. How could I move them? Where could I move them to? Where will I find honest people without children, Frau Porges? I could only move out on a Sunday. Who would carry my cases on a Sunday? It's unfeasible. Surely you wouldn't put me at the mercy of strangers, Frau Porges! It's unfeasible, Frau Porges, unfeasible!'

'You count your things and you think I'm stealing your writing paper. It's true I'm poor, Herr Polzer, but to take other people's property, never, Herr Polzer, never in my life!'

'But I never doubted it, Frau Porges,' he said.

She dabbed her eyes with her handkerchief.

'Sit down, Frau Porges,' said Polzer, 'do sit down. I don't suspect you of stealing, believe me. I don't suspect anyone. Counting everything is a habit of mine, Frau Porges, a habit from the bank, that is all, believe me!'

Frau Porges had sat down. Tearfully she forgave Polzer. It was twenty minutes to eight. Frau Porges was getting more and more worked up. She felt sorry for herself because she was all alone and complained with feeling that a poor widow was defenceless against any insult. She gave free rein to her heartfelt emotion. Polzer looked at the clock in some agitation. It was almost a quarter to. He pointed this out to Frau Porges. In her emotional state, however, she dismissed it as unimportant.

'You'll arrive a bit later this morning,' she said. 'Surely you can see what a state I'm in? Can't I count on your comfort and support, poor lonely widow that I am?'

'You can count on it, Frau Porges,' said Polzer.

'I can?'

She smiled and started to get up.

Polzer straightened up and went rigid.

The clock struck a quarter to. Frau Porges said something, but Polzer didn't hear. He hurried out and still managed to arrive at the bank on time.

When Frau Porges came into Polzer's room that evening he had the feeling she wanted to continue the conversation. Polzer did not raise his eyes from the newspaper. She left, and for the first time Polzer noticed a hostile, angry look in her eyes. The look she gave him still disturbed him during the night, when he was lying in bed.

That summer Polzer could not take his usual walk along the Embankment. He was very fond of that walk. The river was full of people paddling and swimming, rowing-boats and steamboats taking people on day trips. From the islands came the sound of military bands. Polzer used to walk along among families and individuals out for a stroll. A completely unknown face was rare, sometimes it was people from the street where he lived, sometimes a man from the bank or the café. He walked slowly, seeing how his shoes shone in the sun. He trod carefully, so as not to dirty them. Out of fear of thieves, he kept his hands clasped behind his back, over the pocket where he had his wallet. Sometimes he felt a rush of consternation when he sensed a glance directed at him. He quickly looked down to make sure all his buttons were done up. He was aware that his suit was not in the latest fashion and that distressed him. He could not help arousing attention. Children and adolescent girls in particular seemed dangerous and he took great care to avoid them. He walked along in the sunshine as far as the theatre. Then he turned off towards the city centre and went into the café.

These walks ceased now, since immediately after lunch on Sundays Frau Porges would come into his room in her black Sunday dress. He felt it was impossible to go along the Embankment with her, among all those people. Moreover Karl Fanta lived on the Embankment, and he would have to walk past his windows. The memory of Kuchelbad was still too vivid for him to go on another outing with Frau Porges. There was nothing left for it but to go to the café with Frau Porges. He sat with her at the little table in the billiard room.

The first time Polzer came in with Frau Porges, the students leant on their long cues and looked at Frau Porges. Polzer hid behind the newspaper. Frau Porges wanted to talk, but Polzer remained silent. He felt they were being observed from all sides and was afraid their conversation might be overheard at the neighbouring tables.

He was in the café with Frau Porges for the third time when a student came and sat at the table. Frau Porges had met him on the tram. He was tall and slim, had blond hair and the suggestion of a beard.

Frau Porges had a lively conversation with him. She laughed a lot and very loud. Polzer watched the billiard players and took no part in the conversation. He would have liked to ask Frau Porges to moderate her laughter, but found no opportunity. They talked to each other and ignored Polzer. The student accompanied Frau Porges all the way home and said goodbye at the entrance to the apartment block.

Next Sunday the student brought friends to the table. They had to move the chairs up close together. The conversation was noisy. When Polzer looked round the room, he saw that the young man who worked at the table opposite him in the bank was sitting by the window smiling at him. Polzer decided to leave the café at once and stood up. Frau Porges put her hand on his and gave him a pleading look. The young man noticed this and nodded at Polzer. They all started going on at Polzer to persuade him to stay. A fat woman at the next table was observing the animated scene through her lorgnon. Polzer knew who she was. Her husband was a professor at the Weinberg High School. Polzer sat down meekly.

The man sitting next to him, an elegantly dressed young doctor, turned to him. 'What a lucky man you are! To have such an attractive wife!'

Polzer turned to face him. He was searching for suitable words to correct the misunderstanding. But Frau Porges had heard what the doctor had said.

She laughed out loud.

'If only you knew, doctor,' she said, 'if only you knew!'

She looked at Polzer, laughing all the time. Everyone joined in and looked at Polzer. Only the doctor did not laugh.

Polzer noticed that his table had attracted the attention of everyone in the café. He was filled with consternation. The tears of laughter were running down Frau Porges's cheeks. She dried them with her handkerchief.

'Oh Polzer, Polzer,' she said.

That only increased his bewilderment. She had never called him just Polzer before. He felt she was trying to humiliate him. He noticed that the student was stroking the back of her hand and tried to say something. The young man from the bank had stood up and was laughing and nodding at Polzer. Frau Porges put her hand under the table. The student's hand followed. Frau Porges's blouse had slipped. To his horror, Franz Polzer found himself looking down her blouse. He could see the top of her breasts moving. The young man had gone out of the door. Polzer had not acknowledged his nod of farewell. It was too late to hurry after him. He would already have disappeared among all the people in the street.

Frau Porges was talking quietly to the man next to her.

During the night Polzer's rest was disturbed by the thought that at work young Wodak might make remarks about their meeting in the café. Polzer did not know how he should respond to them. Anything that was said about his relationship with the widow that did not correspond to the truth could undermine his position.

When Polzer sat down at his desk next morning, young Wodak was already there. He smiled. Polzer was expecting an attack from Wodak and his own

complete humiliation. But Wodak said nothing. On
the contrary, his behaviour seemed to Polzer to be
more polite and obliging than usual. Polzer calmed
down. He could not know that Wodak had prepared
a specific plan to humiliate him.

That was on the Monday. At the end of the week
something occurred that brought a fundamental
change to Polzer's life. The occurrence was connected
with Polzer's hat.

It was a hard hat, black, with a band of the same colour. The brim was narrow and straight, the crown high. On either side was a small airhole.

The hat had never seemed particularly remarkable to Polzer, even if its brim was scarcely more than a finger's width. Even later, even when he gave it careful thought, he could never see anything special about it. Polzer would stand looking at the window-displays in the hat shops. He saw hats with broader brims and lower crowns. He looked at men he passed in the streets and saw broad-brimmed and narrow-brimmed hats. Hats with high crowns and hats with low crowns. He came across people with hats that ended in a point and had two different-coloured ribbons criss-crossing them. Hats like that seemed special to him. What also struck him was that the hats of people from elsewhere were different from the locals' hats. After a while Polzer could immediately distinguish a visitor to the city by his hat. These hats were similar. Only their colours varied. But they were almost all either black or grey. The brims were always the same width and the crowns the same height. Moreover these hats always looked new.

On the Saturday of that week Polzer was wearing his black hat as he hurried home from the bank. It was seven o'clock in the evening. The streets were full of belated shoppers and office-workers making their way home. The air was full of the noise of shutters sliding down and the bells of the crowded trams. Polzer turned off from Wenceslas Square into Wassergasse and passed two teenage girls.

He had only taken a few more steps when he heard them laugh out loud. He turned round. He didn't know whether they were laughing at him. He realised they were when he saw their faces. Their eyes were fixed on his hat.

Polzer feared that a bird had perhaps done something on his hat. Horrified, he snatched it from his head. He turned it round in his hand and examined it thoroughly. The girls had come up to him. They were laughing out loud. People were gathering round Polzer. He was standing, bareheaded, in the middle of them. More and more people came. It was the busiest street corner.

The crowd was observed from the electric tram. Polzer saw all the faces behind the windows turned towards him. All around, people were smiling. Polzer put his hat back on his head.

The parents of the two girls had arrived. They were large and fat. The father had a dark-coloured soft hat with a tuft of chamois hair in the band. They were visitors to the city. Polzer tried to leave. The girls ran after him. He turned round and found himself standing just in front of them. They were holding each other by the hand and laughing. They were wearing shiny black hats with multi-coloured ribbons. They were emboldened by Polzer's perplexed look.

'O God, o God,' one cried, 'who on earth left you that hat?'

Polzer blushed, for the hat did indeed come from Herr Porges's effects. Frau Porges had had it altered to fit Polzer's head.

'What an antique!' said their father. 'How much do you want for it? I'll make you an offer.'

'I work in a bank,' replied Franz Polzer in embarrassment.

The girls had walked on and the crowd around Polzer dispersed. Polzer put the hat under his arm and hurried home.

He went into his room and put the hat on the table. He examined it closely. He saw that the initials G.P. had been stuck to the leather round the inside. Herr Porges had been called Gottlieb. Until now Polzer had not noticed the initials. He felt that his embarrassment out in the street, which had exposed him to the mocking looks of all those passing by, was the result of a malicious trick on the part of the late Herr Porges and his widow, Klara, who were out to humiliate him. He recalled the angry expression in Frau Porges's eyes. It was immediately clear to him that she, who had left him helpless at the mercy of passers-by from all sides, was perfectly capable of carrying out her threat to take his room away from him. He removed the two letters from the leather lining and placed them on the table beside the hat.

When Frau Porges came in she noticed the hat at once. She saw the letters as well. She gave Polzer a questioning look.

Polzer said calmly, 'I will not wear the hat again, Frau Porges.'

'You won't? Such a good hat? My late husband

had it for so long and hardly ever wore it. He was laid up in bed most of the time.'

'I refuse, Frau Porges,' said Polzer.

'You refuse? What?'

'To wear the hat of your late husband, Frau Porges. I refuse to inherit things from your late husband, Frau Porges, absolutely refuse.'

'Absolutely?'

Polzer realised she was talking about the room.

'As far as the hat is concerned, Frau Porges, only as far as the hat is concerned.'

Frau Porges smiled and sat down.

'What has happened, Herr Polzer,' she said.

Polzer described the incident in the street.

'I will never wear this hat again,' he concluded. Frau Porges stood up. She took the hat and looked at it.

'A beautiful hat. Almost new. There'd be no problem selling it . . . You'll go to Bunzl's in Schulgasse tomorrow, in the morning. Tomorrow's Sunday. You'll sell the hat,' she decreed and left the room.

He ran out to discuss it with her.

It was already dark in the kitchen. The light was on in Frau Porges's bedroom. Polzer stood in the dark hallway. Through the glass in the door he could see Frau Porges's shadow moving. Then the light went out in Frau Porges's room.

Polzer stood in the hall for a while, waiting. Then he went back into his own room. His supper was still on the table, untouched. He had not read the newspaper yet, either. On top of all that, he could not compose himself. He had to know whether he would have to go to Bunzl's in the morning to sell the hat, or whether Frau Porges would relent. Tomorrow was Sunday, so he could go in the morning. But in that case there were preparations to be made. The hat had to be wrapped up. And if he did have to take it, then perhaps the initials should be stuck back on the leather. They were part of it really.

Polzer could not allow things to reach a point where Frau Porges gave him notice to quit his room because of this affair. He realised that she was justifiably angry with him. She could not but see his rejection of the hat as an insult to her late husband. There was no doubt that she was seriously considering making him leave. She had gone out of the room without waiting for an answer. If she gave him notice in the morning, he would have to find a new room by the first. He was well aware that thefts frequently occurred during removals. He imagined how difficult it must be to keep a watch on the removal men who, anyway, were coarse and recalcitrant. Polzer was horrified at the thought of all his things that would have to be packed. He would not be able to count on any help from Frau Klara Porges. He would wrap the picture of St. Francis in paper and carry it in his hand. The idea of having to find another room made him particularly agitated. In which district should he look first? The city was large, it was impossible to know where to begin. Moreover, rooms were difficult to find and the landlord might be dishonest. Also there might be children living there.

Polzer went to bed. But he could not get to sleep.

He knew that all this agitation would be too much for him. Perhaps he would fall ill and have to be absent from the bank. The work would pile up on his desk. A new stack came every day. When he returned, it would have grown to a huge mountain. Then Polzer would probably collapse completely. It was dark in the room, but there was a creaking noise. Polzer held his breath. Perhaps Frau Porges was turning over and it was her bed that was creaking. The walls were so thin. Perhaps Frau Porges was not asleep either.

Polzer didn't dare move, but there was still a loud creaking. This time it was definitely in his room. Something was happening. Should he not after all go and see if Frau Porges was awake, knock gently on her door? Perhaps she would forgive him for insulting her late husband if he agreed to atone for it by taking the hat to the shop. Perhaps she had not really meant it seriously. Perhaps it would be best anyway if the hat were sold. He certainly wasn't going to wear it again.

There was not a gleam of light anywhere. Polzer would have liked to put the light on, but he didn't dare turn the switch. He knew it would be better to pretend to be asleep. Polzer could sense the danger. He stretched out his hand cautiously to feel for the picture of St. Francis. His arm moved slowly. It was a long time before it was fully stretched. His muscles were aching. His arm was trembling. But the picture was still there. He touched the edge of its wooden frame. He decided not to take his hand away at once, he would to leave it resting on the picture, just for a second. Then he would slowly and inaudibly withdraw his hand.

The saint fell. It fell onto the wooden headboard, rending the silence. Polzer's eyes bulged. He could have held the picture there, but he did not move. His arm remained stretching up. The picture seemed to wobble. Then it fell again. It fell on the floor. The glass splintered. The sudden clatter confused Polzer. The noise rebounded terrifyingly from the dark walls. Polzer leapt up and ran out of the room.

He stopped outside the door to Frau Polzer's room.

Polzer was wearing his nightshirt. His body was damp with sweat. He was trembling. Frau Porges must have heard the noise. Polzer knocked softly on the door. She did not answer. Polzer knocked again.

'Who's there?' asked Frau Porges.

'Me, Polzer,' he replied.

'Herr Polzer? What is it, Herr Polzer?'

He heard her get out of bed and approach the door. He grasped the door-handle in his hand and held the door tight shut.

'Stay there, Frau Porges,' said Polzer, 'stay there. I just wanted to ask your forgiveness, that's all. Stay there, I'm not properly dressed, Frau Porges.'

Frau Porges pressed down the door-handle. Polzer held the door shut. His teeth grated on each other.

'I ask your forgiveness for that too, but you can't open the door. I'm not properly dressed, Frau Porges. I was already in bed. But about tomorrow, about the hat, I just wanted to tell you that I can go, if you like. But you have to tell me the price, how much you want for it, and whether I should stick the letters back on the leather.'

She overcame his resistance and opened the door.

In the dark he could see that her hair was hanging down.

She was in her nightdress too.

She took him by the hand.

'Come, Polzer,' she said. Her voice sounded deep. 'Come!'

He did not move.

She pulled him into the dark room and closed the door. Then she led him to the bed.

'You're trembling,' she said.

The bed was warm. She pulled the quilt over him. The bed smelt of hair. Frau Porges lay down beside him.

'You're not going to give me notice, Frau Porges?' he said.

She laughed and snuggled up against him. He realised that now she expected something of him. Polzer drew very close to her. Frau Porges felt Polzer and laughed out loud. Polzer thought of the possibility of being given notice and made every effort. He grew more agitated and more impatient by the second. He noticed that there were beads of sweat on his brow. Now Frau Porges just lay there, not moving.

'Aren't you sweating, my little trembler,' she said with a laugh, 'aren't you just sweating!'

Polzer immediately felt ashamed, even though he knew it was quite natural and no disgrace.

'I'm tired,' said Frau Porges. She yawned and

stretched. Then she turned to the wall. 'And you woke me just for that?'

She laughed. 'Perhaps you'll manage it tomorrow.'

She had turned her back to Polzer. He felt humiliated. He knew that now he ought to get up and go to his room. St. Francis was on the floor in his room. He was afraid Frau Porges would demand he leave her room, if he did not get up at once to return to his bed and spend the rest of the night listening to the noises that came out of the darkness. But Frau Porges's breathing was already deep and regular. Polzer lay on the edge of the bed. He drew up his feet so the widow would not notice his presence. Carefully he covered himself over with one corner of the quilt.

It was morning when Polzer got up and went to his room. Frau Porges was still asleep. He had got out of bed quietly. In his room the picture of St. Francis was on the floor. He picked it up, cleaned off the splinters of glass and hung it back in its place on the wall.

Polzer sat down by the window and started to clean his shoes. He watched how, with every stroke of the brush, the rays of the sun were reflected more and more brightly in the black leather.

He heard steps in the adjoining room. He did not want to see Frau Porges. He wrapped the hat in paper and crept cautiously out of the apartment.

That Sunday afternoon Polzer accompanied Frau Porges to the café again. Of the young people, only the blond student and the black-haired doctor were sitting at their table. Frau Porges sat beside the student. Polzer paid no attention to them. He talked to the doctor. The doctor expressed his amazement that Polzer had retained so much of what he had learnt. He said he envied Polzer his memory. He also showed interest in the bank and told Polzer he too had once considered the idea of working in a bank. Polzer, for his part, praised the study of medicine and the medical profession, which had been his ambition in his youth. For all that, he went on, he had to admit that his present profession had its advantages too, above all in providing a secure livelihood independent of age and sickness.

Polzer was pleased at the interest the other showed. He learnt that the doctor was called Heinrich Ehrmann. He was comfortably off and did not practise his profession.

Polzer's handkerchief fell on the floor. He bent down to pick it up. Then Polzer saw that the blond student had his hand on Frau Porges's knee. Polzer recoiled with a start. At that moment something terrible happened. The door opened wide and about ten colleagues from the bank appeared, led by young Wodak. They laughed as they greeted him and sat down at the neighbouring table. Among them were three from correspondence, several from accounts and one from foreign exchange. There was even a head clerk with them. They sat at the next table, scrutinising Frau Porges and laughing across at them.

Polzer stood up. He gave them a frozen smile. Frau Porges had also got up.

Not a word was said on the way home. The student and the doctor had stayed in the café. At home Frau Porges changed out of her suit. Then she came into Polzer's room. She was wearing a blouse that hung down loose over her waist, like Milka's blouse.

Polzer said, 'I can't go back to the bank.' His voice was trembling. 'They all saw me.'

Frau Porges smiled.

Polzer said, 'When the student had his hand on your knee, Frau Porges . . .'

She came up close to him. He saw how broad and fat she was. Her breasts hung down. There were dark hairs on her cheeks.

He could feel her warm breath.

Her breasts under the loose blouse were already touching his body. He raised his hands to ward them off, but his fingers dug themselves firmly into the heavy mass of flesh.

That evening he did manage it.

She had switched off the light and was asleep beside him. Her arm was underneath his shoulders.

During the night Franz Polzer was seized by an immense and terrible thought, beyond comprehension.

It happened all of a sudden. The white line of her

parting was a pale shimmer. It was as if her body were soft and dark. He reached out for that body. And it suddenly came to him that it was the body of his sister.

He knew quite well the idea was without foundation. He had never had a sister. But the thought was there, and too immense for him to try to drive it away.

Franz Polzer got up, wrapped himself in his coat and sat down at the table. He felt as if he had had sexual relations with his sister. He recalled the nights at home when the rotten floorboards creaked under his father's heavy footsteps and he, seized with horror, lay in bed, listening.

At ten o'clock colleagues from all departments appeared in the room where Franz Polzer was. That was the time when the noise of the machines was silent for a few minutes.

Polzer bent over his work and did not look up. His colleagues congratulated him, laughing.

'Who would have thought it?' said one from accounts. 'Still waters.'

'D'you think he can satisfy her, gentlemen? Isn't he too weak and skinny for her?'

'Don't say that,' said the head clerk. He gave a superior smile. He was experienced in such matters. 'That woman knows what she's doing. You can believe me. They say the skinniest cocks are the best, and not without reason.'

'Nevertheless, sir,' said Fogl, 'with a window display like that she must squash him flat against the wall when she turns over in bed.'

'We would like to become acquainted with the lady, Herr Polzer,' said the head clerk. 'As our colleague you owe us that, Herr Polzer. I propose we all go on an outing together this Sunday afternoon. You have no objection to that, have you, Herr Polzer?'

Polzer said nothing.

'Come now, won't you say yes, Herr Polzer?'

Polzer nodded. He had not slept the previous night and had slipped out of the apartment before Frau Porges woke up. He was afraid of returning there in the evening. He thought of going to see Fanta, telling him everything and asking him to take him in, at least for one night. But Karl would not understand. It was something that was impossible even to say, because it was so far beyond comprehension.

Young Wodak handed a sheaf of paper over to him and smiled. They all smiled and did not understand.

He could not go home that evening. Frau Porges would be waiting for him. Perhaps she would already be sitting in his room when he got back. Better to go and see Karl Fanta, find some pretext to stay longer. Only get back home after Frau Porges was asleep. But in that case perhaps she would be lying in his bed, prepared for him, and he would not be able to escape her.

On the other hand, Frau Porges might be angry with him, might order him to leave her apartment. Then there would be nothing for it but to pack his things in his suitcase and go. To have to take a room with strangers, perhaps with thieves, and that only after an endless, exhausting search, up and down stairs, through every district of the city. Oh, to take everything upon himself, in his bed under the picture of St. Francis, to accept it, like the blows from his father in the dark kitchen, while his aunt held him. She screamed, but he was silent because that was the way it was, the way it had to be, in that house, with that shop. It was impossible to escape. Impossible to escape Milka's hands, the creak on the stairs, the parting in his aunt's hair, his father's fleshy, naked chest with the tangle of grey and red hair under his gaping nightshirt, impossible to escape Klara, her parting, the bristly hairs on her cheeks, her warm body in the bed.

The air was stuffy in the small room, his hands were damp from his work and his fingers left marks on the paper. It was not permitted to open the window because the door was never still and it would create a draught that would blow the loose sheets off their desks. The large, packed building with all its big and small rooms echoed to the sound of talking, of steps constantly going up and down stairs and along corridors, of the never-ceasing clatter of the blue letters popping up from the machines onto the white paper. It was shortly before six when Polzer could resist no longer and closed his eyes. He was not asleep. He continued to hear the noise echoing round the building, young Wodak turning over one sheet of paper after another. But at the same time he felt he could not distinguish the individual sounds from each other. All at once they were immensely loud, close and dangerous. They all merged, growing into a turbulent hubbub of voices. Polzer opened his eyes.

The colleagues who had been there in the morning were in the room, ready to leave, looking at him and smiling. Polzer stood up and took his hat. His colleagues were in a good mood and reminded him of the outing on Sunday. It was quite understandable, they felt, that Polzer had fallen asleep. Franz Polzer found himself staring at the laughing face of the head clerk. It seemed fatter than usual. The head clerk was wearing a new tie and a lightweight check suit. Polzer noticed that his own black bow-tie had slipped and was underneath his ear. In spite of all his efforts he could not pull it back into place. He left the room and ran down the stairs. He heard his colleagues' laughter and was ashamed that they, in their good clothes and newly soled shoes, were laughing at his suit. He realised that the head clerk had found him asleep. He might report it to the management. He would have to see the head clerk in the morning and ask him not to do so, as it was the first time it had happened.

When Polzer opened the door and stepped out into the street, he found Frau Porges there.

She had been waiting for him.

He could hear the steps of his colleagues on the stairs. He took Frau Porges by the arm.

'Come on,' he said, 'come on.'

He dragged her away quickly. They mustn't see that Frau Porges had been waiting for him.

'What's the hurry?' asked Frau Porges.

He did not reply.

'Why did you run off this morning?' she said.

He avoided her eye and looked at the ground.

She laughed. 'Just like a schoolboy,' she said, 'just like a schoolboy. Perhaps you should be beaten like a boy.'

It gave Polzer a great shock.

'To make you obey,' she said.

He quickly ate the supper she brought him. Then he bolted his door and went to bed.

Frau Porges came and tried to open it. When she realised it was bolted, she knocked. 'Open up, Polzer,' she shouted. Then, when he did not obey immediately, 'Open up!'

Franz Polzer got up and opened the door.

Frau Porges was wearing just her vest and a black petticoat.

'You weren't happy with me, I suppose,' she said.

She came up close to him. He tried to back away, but she grasped him by the wrist.

On the chair was the belt he used for his trousers. She picked it up.

'Take off your nightshirt,' she commanded.

He held it tight with both hands. She pulled it away from him.

'Drop the nightshirt!'

He threw his nightshirt onto the floor.

He put his thin arms over his body to hide his sunken chest and flabby belly. He was ashamed to expose this body.

He did not move and kept his eyes half closed. He waited.

He heard her burst out laughing. He flinched at her laugh. Then he heard the swish of the belt.

Klara Porges had raised the belt and brought it down. She hit him with the end where the buckle was attached. He raised his thin arms to protect himself. She pushed him onto the bed so that he was lying face down.

'Now you will obey,' she said.

She got into bed with him, naked. Her hair had come undone. It was hanging over her shoulders.

She arranged her body for him. Polzer did not move. Her body glistened with the dampness of sweat. Above her eyes was her parting. The white skin shone through. Her fat breasts had slumped to the side and lay there, limp, before him.

The bed grew warm from her. He felt his body grow damp with her heat as well. She was horribly exposed and open. Only her head was not exposed. On it was his aunt's parting, still intact.

Franz Polzer did not move. The thought that had come yesterday was back again, and more vivid than it had been the previous day.

Frau Porges pushed him out of the bed so that he fell heavily on the floor. He took his nightshirt and covered himself with it.

During the night he woke. He could feel that Frau Porges's hands had pulled his nightshirt up and were groping his body.

The bed was low and the hands could reach him easily. He could not see Frau Porges; just her arms stuck out from the bed.

He turned his head to one side. He closed his eyes. Now he was certain what was to come. He trembled, as he had done on the stairs at the touch of Milka's hands.

She gave him a push and laughed. He breathed deeply.

He waited the whole night for her to feel for him again. Towards morning she felt for him a second time.

From the bank Franz Polzer went straight to Karl Fanta's. It was Tuesday.

Karl was sitting in an armchair which had been drawn up to the window.

'Tuesday!' he cried, as Franz Polzer entered.

Franz Polzer pulled a chair over to the window. 'How are you?' he asked timidly.

Karl laughed. 'Brilliant question! How am I?! But then you've never suffered from excessive intelligence. That's not meant as an insult, Franz. Just a statement of fact. How am I, with no legs, and abscesses on my arms? Fine, my dear Franz, just fine!' He laughed and gave Franz a malevolent look through his large horn-rimmed spectacles.

Franz Polzer was silent. He was used to these outbursts from Karl which he feared and could not prevent. Recently Karl had started talking a lot, almost uninterruptedly. It was as if he was afraid of a break in the conversation.

'But you, my dear Polzer, how are you? You're still in the thick of things, the social whirl, aren't you? Ha, ha! And what's your Frau Klara Porges doing? What a name, eh? Really! Is she still putting on weight, your widow? And can you satisfy her, Polzer? I wouldn't have great confidence in you.'

'Oh come now,' said Polzer, 'you know that my relations with her are purely formal. I rent a room from her. She comes from a respectable family.'

Karl Fanta laughed out loud. 'From a respectable family! Franz, Franz, these Tuesdays do brighten up my life. From a respectable family! Young girls from respectable families . . .' He stopped laughing. 'I want to see her, your respectable Frau Klara Porges, Polzer. I've already asked you.'

'She's completely lacking in education,' said Polzer. 'What do you want with her?'

'Shhh!' said Karl Fanta, and leant forward in his chair. 'They mustn't hear. I have to see her. I have to get away from here!'

'Get away from here?' asked Polzer, horrified. 'You? Why?'

Karl Fanta glanced at the door. 'They hate me,' he said quietly. His eyes flickered. 'They want me dead!'

'Who?' Polzer jumped to his feet. 'You dead? Who?'

'She does! Don't look so disbelieving. She wants me dead. She wants to be free. And she's afraid of me, that's another reason.'

'Dora?'

'Dora! I looked different when she married me. Now I'm lying here with no legs. A rump. My arms already covered in abscesses. The palms of my hands are always sweaty, even though I do nothing. And this belly's getting fatter and fatter, swollen like a blown-up sack. And the revolting business with my stools! I want a male nurse, Polzer, a paid nurse, d'you hear, but she won't allow it, she refuses to let my dying body out of her sight. She thinks I might recover after all. She just can't stand it.'

'Dora can't stand it?'

'I can't stand it, Polzer, I can't! She's a model of patience, takes it like a little lamb. Can you imagine it? What devotion, people say. Bandages my stinking sores. "Can you smell the stench?" I ask her, but she just smiles sweetly, as if she can't smell it. "You're keeping your face well away," I say. "You can't stand it, Dora dear, sweetheart," I say. Then she puts her lips so close you'd think she was going to kiss the pus. I can see clearly that she smiles and doesn't pull a face and takes an audible, deep breath, as if it were roses she was smelling. But I can see through it, I can see through it, Polzer. I'm sure she goes out and spews. I disgust her. But she's clever, oh she's clever. "I can wait," she thinks. "It can't be long now. No point in getting worked up, arguing, screaming." Hah! What I wouldn't do to spoil her little game! I can hardly grow another pair of legs, but I could stay alive, the way I am, unable to move, stinking, sweating, fat. Just to spite her, d'you understand, Polzer, just to spite her. She thinks if I had a nurse I wouldn't need her any more. The fact that I haven't forces me to be careful not to make her angry. I have to be nice to her, smile, so that she doesn't walk out on me. I can't tell her what I know. There'd be no point, it wouldn't do any good. She'd stick me by the window here in the morning and leave me here all day. When I have a nurse, Polzer, I'll get him to wheel me into all the rooms, all the time. Nothing will escape my notice. I'll be here, there and everywhere. Then I'll tell her everything I know, Polzer, everything. And then I'll leave this place.'

'Where will you go, Karl?'

'To live with you, perhaps; perhaps to live with you. Let me have a look at your widow. I like to see fat women. I used to like them skinnier, I suppose, but not any more, Polzer. Dora's as skinny as a child, Polzer. Tiny breasts, hardly anything to get your hands on.'

'Don't talk like that, Karl,' said Polzer.

'Huh! I shouldn't talk like that, should I? I should be ashamed of myself, should I? Because she has such a well-developed sense of shame? Do you know she goes with other men? Well may you shake your head, Polzer. You know all about that, don't you, you with your experience, with your knowledge of women? You old Casanova, eh? "Don't talk like that, Karl."' He imitated Polzer's voice. 'I'll talk like that because you're that kind of fellow.

D'you know what I do, Polzer? Every evening? I'll tell you. I order her to get undressed. The first time, she refused. "What's he after?" she thought, "That stump's not a man any more." And she was right. "Dora, sweetheart," I said, "I want to see you again, like I did in the old days," I said, in that pleading voice, you know. "I know I'm not a man any more. But still," I said, "do it for me, Dora, sweetheart." I looked at her and she did it. As if she were still a girl of fourteen. "Dora," I said, "come close to me." I can't lift my hands. "Bend down, Dora," I said, "I want to feel your breasts in my hands, Dora." She didn't move. "Why not?" I said. "Have I stopped being your husband because I'm so ill? Five years ago you let me, because I could do everything, and now, because I can't do anything any more apart from

71

stroke your breasts, you won't let me do even that?"
So then she came right up to me and bent down until
her breasts touched my hands. But I could see it
made her feel ashamed. Why wasn't she ashamed
before? Ha! What would she not do, and allow me to
do to her, without feeling ashamed! And now all at
once she felt ashamed. She was almost in tears. Do
you know why she felt ashamed, Polzer, why she was
crying? Because I'm so unhappy? No, no, I don't
believe that. She feels ashamed because she has to let
herself be touched by me, by someone who isn't a
man any more. She feels ashamed to have her breasts
touched like things by a thing! I'm a thing, Polzer, a
thing. Now I do it almost every day, Polzer, every
day. She'll see what kind of husband she has, Polzer,
even if it makes her hate me! The next time you
come, Polzer, I'll call her. I'll let you watch, Polzer.
I want you to see how much she loves me.'

Polzer was horrified at the sight of Karl's face,
which was twisted in a frozen grin. He looked away,
out of the window, at the river and the green hills on
the other side.

Karl Fanta sank back in his armchair. Talking,
even in a low voice, had made him tired.

'A glass of water,' he said.

Polzer handed it to him.

Karl Fanta drank.

Then he gripped Polzer's sleeve. 'She brings men
into the house,' he said. 'I can't stop her. I have to
leave, Polzer,' he said.

'Karl, Karl, how can you think that,' said Polzer.
He was bewildered and did not know what to say.

'I have my suspicions,' said Karl Fanta, giving Franz Polzer a look, 'well-founded suspicions.'

Franz Polzer started back. 'Not of me?' he asked in alarm.

Karl let go of him. 'Of you? Hahaha! Fool! Of you!'

'Who are you suspicious of, then?'

'Of her!' He paused and listened. Then he went on, softly, 'go and have a look, Polzer. There's someone listening at the door.'

Polzer went to have a look. There was no one listening at the door.

'I'm sitting here. She's washed, fed and bandaged me. The boy's at school, the cook's in the kitchen, the maid's out shopping. She's in one of the back rooms. Suddenly doors open, footsteps, yes, someone's come. Sometimes I hear whispering, very soft, if you didn't know you wouldn't hear it. He's there, with her, Polzer.'

'Who?'

'Who? Perhaps a friend who at other times comes to visit me, perhaps the janitor, the butcher, the baker's boy. Perhaps a different one every day. Ten minutes have passed, they could be at it by now. So I ring. And she comes. Calm, unflustered, only the slightest of flushes on her cheeks. She's presumably run a comb through her hair. "Dora, sweetheart," I say, "I've had enough of being on my own." I look her straight in the eye as I say it. "Forget your chores in the back, Dora. Get a book and read to me." She sits down and reads. I make her read for an hour. Let him sweat it out in the back there, I don't take my eyes off her for one second. "That's enough," I say. "I'm tired now. Perhaps I'll have a little sleep. You go off back to what you were doing." She shuts the book and goes. I don't care if she hates me even more. Perhaps they'll kill me, the two of them. Poison me. I'm ill and no one would suspect. You have to help me, Polzer! You'll bring her next Thursday, won't you? Your Klara?'

'What should I say to Dora?'

'That you want to introduce her to me. Say she asked you to. Bring her, bring her, Polzer!'

Before he left he went into Franz's room.

Franz Fanta handed him his homework so that Polzer could do it for him. Polzer ran his fingers through the boy's dark hair.

'You must have it done by tomorrow, Polzer,' said Franz Fanta. 'And don't put any mistakes in. I'll come and collect it tomorrow. Make sure it's ready, Polzer, d'you hear?'

Dora was in the doorway. 'Franz!' she said. 'What a way to speak is that?! Herr Polzer's too good to you. He gives up his time for you and you take it as a matter of course.'

'Please, Polzer,' said Franz, 'don't forget.'

He sat down again and went back to the book he had been reading when Polzer came in. 'My best wishes to Frau Porges,' he said.

Polzer went out into the corridor. Dora followed him.

'I have to talk to you, Herr Polzer,' she said. 'Just wait a moment, I'll get my hat and walk with you.'

74

They went down the stairs in silence. Dora was pale and anxious.

'He only thinks of himself,' she said when they were out of the building. 'But isn't he a handsome boy? They say Karl looked just like that when he was fifteen.'

'He did?' said Polzer. They were walking along the side of the road closest to the river. It was getting cold and night was falling, but there were still boats gliding over the water.

'He did?' Polzer repeated, coming to a halt. He looked at Dora, who was avoiding his eye. He was amazed that it had never occurred to him before. Now he remembered.

'He did!' he said.

He looked at the river. Suddenly Dora took his hand. Polzer turned round. He was looking at an anxious face.

'Did he tell you, Polzer?' she asked.

'Tell me what?' Polzer asked.

She had let go of his hand and was grasping the iron railing that separated the road from the river. The tears shone in her big black eyes.

'He's tormenting me, he's tormenting me,' she said softly.

Polzer was silent for a moment. After a while he said, 'You should take a male nurse to look after him.'

'No, no!' cried Dora, 'I can't do that. That would really set him off. He would say I didn't love him, that I'd taken a nurse on so I could spend all my time with my . . . o God, o God, Herr Polzer . . . That I find his sores nauseating, hasn't he told you that, Herr Polzer? No, I can't take on a nurse, Herr Polzer, or all hell would be let loose. And now, you know, he wants to leave, Herr Polzer, to go and live with you. You're the only one, he says, you've known him since you were children, you'd take him in. Did he tell you that?'

'He did hint at it, Frau Fanta.'

'And do you know why? The idea would never occur to him in the normal run of things. It's just to torment me, Herr Polzer, that's all. He wouldn't really want to leave, especially as he loves Franz so much. But he'd do it all the same, just to torment me.'

For a moment she was silent. Then she grasped both of Polzer's hands and looked him straight in the eye. He looked away and kept his eyes fixed to the ground.

'You can prevent it,' she said. 'That's why I've come with you. To ask you not to let it happen.'

'What must I do?' asked Polzer.

'Advise him not to. Tell him to stay with me. Anything but leave! I couldn't bear the scandal. People would say I treated him badly because he was ill. And what would I tell our boy, Herr Polzer. Let him go on tormenting me, if he must! Oh, you don't know what I'm going through.'

She began to sob out loud. Polzer looked round. A man who was walking past on the other side of the street turned to look at them.

'Calm down, Frau Fanta,' said Polzer. 'There are people here.'

She lifted up her face. A lock of hair had come loose and hung in a black curve across her cheek. She looked at him. He felt she expected him to help her. He didn't know what to say.

'Doesn't he love you any more?' he asked after a pause, uncertain whether the question might not make Dora cry again.

She shrugged her shoulders. 'Sometimes I feel he must still love me. What other explanation is there for all this? Do you know what the trouble is?' She came so close to him that he could feel her breath warm on his cheek. 'He doesn't have a heart any more. His heart has been eaten away by ulcers too. That's why he's so cruel to me.'

She kept her eyes fixed on him. He felt that, to her, this explanation for all her suffering was something mysterious, the fruit of long and hard reflection, which one could not contradict.

'Yes,' she said once more, 'he is very cruel to me.'

'And you love him?' he asked

'I loved him very much,' she replied. 'He was so handsome, don't you remember? When he came back from Italy and asked for my hand. So slim and bronzed. Only his eyes looked tired even then. If only one could have foreseen all this,' she said in a subdued voice.

'You wouldn't have accepted him if you had known all this?'

'No – No!' she exclaimed, turning her head in all directions as if looking for help. 'If I had known . . . But the doctors said he had completely recovered in Italy. And after one year, that was it. Think back.

77

The left foot first, one abscess after another. No, no, if I had known, Herr Polzer, how can you ask!? But I didn't, and things being the way they are, you must understand.'

He didn't know what he was being asked to understand.

She was breathing heavily. She seemed to have forgotten him. He did not move. Dora stared at the river.

She turned round and held out her hand. 'Forgive me,' she said softly.

He raised his hat, but she was already crossing the road and disappearing into the entrance of the apartment block.

Polzer hurried home. He was agitated, perturbed. There were changes on the way here and their final outcome could not be foreseen. If the invalid came to live with him, which room would Frau Porges put him in? Presumably not in the one with the good furniture. In the end he, Polzer, would have to move into her room, sleep bed by bed with her all the time. What would he be letting himself in for there! He could still hear Dora's sobbing. If Karl did move out, she might end up doing things that could spread confusion and consternation. When she had stared so fixedly at the water he had the feeling she was thinking of death. He was to take Frau Porges with him next Tuesday. Perhaps that was a good thing, however embarrassing he found it. It seemed unlikely to him that Frau Porges would be happy with Karl Fanta's plan of moving in with them. And perhaps she would be able to persuade Frau Fanta to take on a male nurse. It was always possible that the two women might get on well together. He resolved to tell Frau Porges all about it when a suitable opportunity arose. In one respect it was comforting to know he would not be going to Karl Fanta's by himself next time: the presence of Frau Porges would protect him from Karl's and Dora's hysterical confessions, which left him totally at a loss. The widow would stay calm and perhaps she would set things right again.

Since Franz was coming to collect his homework the next day, Polzer got up early in the morning. He wrote out the exercises neatly on sheets of white foolscap without a single crossing-out. That evening he hurried home from the bank so as not to be late for Franz. He heard his voice in the kitchen. Polzer went to his room. He waited for Franz to come to him. He had deliberately closed the door noisily and cleared his throat in the hall, so that they could hear in the kitchen that he had arrived home.

Polzer had been restlessly walking up and down in his room for about a quarter of an hour before Franz came in.

Polzer gave him the homework. Franz glanced at it quickly.

'No mistakes in it, Polzer?'

'I believe there are no mistakes in it. How is your father, Franz?'

'God,' said Franz, 'my father! I don't think Father's ever going to get any better, do you?'

'We must never give up hope, Franz.'

'Yes, yes . . . Tell me, Polzer, they say I look like

Father used to look. Do you think I might get ill like him some day?'

Polzer drew the boy to him and pressed his head against his breast. He was moved by Franz Fanta's question. For a moment his hand lay on Franz's soft hair. He pulled it away quickly, alarmed at the blur of memories of the boy's father, of homework from their *Book of Exercises*, of tears and distant caresses.

'You will certainly not get ill,' he said.

'He torments us,' said Franz, 'Mother and me. Mother thinks you could help us.'

Polzer held Franz tight. He could feel his slender limbs against his body, could feel the rise and fall of Franz's chest as he breathed.

The boy looked at Franz Polzer.

Polzer evaded his eye. He could feel the throb of the boy's pulse. Dora was right. This was a face he had seen. Forgotten similarities filled him with consternation and alarm.

Franz Fanta said, 'Do you love me, Polzer.'

With a horrified start Franz Polzer let go of the boy.

The outing took place on Sunday. Frau Porges had also invited the blond student, the doctor and Kamilla. Kamilla was Frau Porges's childhood friend. She was the wife of a shopkeeper in the Kohlmarkt.

Hanging in his wardrobe Polzer had a short, black frock coat, which he had last worn to his father's funeral. He chose the coat for the outing. On his head he put his soft Panama hat, on his feet he was wearing yellow shoes. They were his best clothes.

They met at the Powder Tower. Of his colleagues from the bank only the head clerk and Herr Fogl turned up. The others had gone to the football match. They were members of the football club.

The head clerk was wearing shorts and knee-length socks. He waved from afar as soon as he saw Frau Porges and Polzer coming. He looked in high spirits and smiled as he ran his eye over Polzer's formal dress. Polzer realised he was wearing the wrong clothes. Immediately he felt dejected. Herr Fogl was wearing a light-coloured suit and a matching hat.

'You're dressed as if for a christening,' said Herr Fogl. They all laughed and looked at Polzer.

They went down Elisabethstrasse, across the bridge, then along the river bank and through more streets to the Arboretum. They were heading for Troja. Walking made Polzer hot. The sun was hot and his coat was heavy. He carried his hat in his hand and lagged behind the others.

Initially the head clerk had tried to attach himself to Frau Porges, who was with the student. Then he turned his attention to Kamilla. The women were wearing light blouses and dark skirts. Kamilla was walking beside Fogl, the widow was recounting some story. Her laugh was loud and deep, like a man's.

The head clerk was making jokes, too, and looking round to see if everyone had heard. He turned to Polzer, who was walking beside the doctor.

'Well, Herr Polzer, and what have you to say about the young man up there with Frau Porges? They look as if they don't want to be disturbed, what?'

'Herr Polzer knows,' said Fogl with a wink, 'that she'll soon be keen to get back to the fleshpots. And anyway, variety is the spice of life, isn't it,' he added, turning to Kamilla.

Kamilla lowered her gaze. 'Oh, you are awful, Herr Fogl,' said Kamilla. She gave his hand a gentle squeeze.

This success raised Herr Fogl's spirits even more and he took the liberty of slipping his arm under Kamilla's. The head clerk did the same on the other side.

Polzer, however, had noticed a hole three or four inches above the knee of the trousers he had not worn for such a long time. It was about the shape and size of a small coin and his white underwear could be seen shining through. Polzer was horrified and placed his hat over the spot. From then on he held it there, hiding the hole, for the rest of the afternoon. He resolved to take Frau Porges to task for it. Clearly she was not looking after his clothes carefully enough, allowing the moths to eat up his possessions. As soon as he got back he would have to subject all his cupboards and wardrobes to a thorough inspection. He saw now that frequent counting could reveal theft, but not other types of loss. It was quite possible that constant attack by moths might render his clothes and underwear unwearable, might perhaps even, since he had never considered the possibility, already have. This thought occupied his mind all the way to Troja and caused him such concern that he took no notice of all the other people who, like him, were also out for a walk, nor responded to the doctor's frequent attempts to start up a conversation.

Nevertheless, this outing was to assume importance for Franz Polzer because of a conversation he had with the doctor. But that did not take place until it was dark, on the way back.

In Troja they stopped at an inn. They ordered wine, butter and cold sausage. Herr Fogl stood up to make a witty toast to the ladies. Kamilla kept giving first Herr Fogl, then the head clerk reproachful looks, but put up no resistance when both gentlemen embraced her. Polzer noticed that Klara Porges and the student drank to each other and that, as in the café, the student had put his hand on hers.

Suddenly they realised that Klara Porges and the student had disappeared. They all laughed and looked at Polzer. Polzer blushed. The men insisted Polzer go and look for the couple. After quite some time he found them in some thick bushes behind the inn. They were looking for forget-me-nots. Polzer knew that there were no forget-me-nots out at that time of the year and pointed out to them that their search was futile.

When it grew dark the conversations ceased. Someone had given Polzer a cigar. He sat there quietly, smoking his cigar. Even the doctor, who was sitting beside him, was silent. The chair on Polzer's left was empty.

Suddenly Polzer sensed movement in the empty chair and a presence. From the rustle of clothes and the body heat, he realised it was a woman. He recognised Kamilla. Her eyes were shining with excitement, her hair was dishevelled. Her face came close up to his.

'Those two are boring,' she said in a whisper. 'They paw you as if you were some animal they'd hired just for the purpose. You're not like that, Herr Polzer. You don't keep patting and pinching a woman like those clumsy oafs.'

Polzer said nothing.

'I know that from Klara,' said Kamilla. She was very close to him and had put her hot hand on Polzer's thigh.

Polzer started and drew back.

'She told me everything,' whispered Kamilla.

'Told you everything?' mumbled Polzer.

She was as fat as Klara Porges, but much shorter. Her hair had been combed up into a high wave at the front, her big eyes were underlined in black.

'Klara told me everything,' she whispered again.

He moved his chair back. 'You're afraid of me? Don't keep moving away.'

Her hand was still on his thigh. He wanted to free himself from that hot hand and pull his leg away. She grasped him tighter.

'Let me,' she whispered against his ear. Her breath smelt of wine. 'Just let me. She's told me everything.'

Then Polzer let out a long, deep groan. It sounded like a suppressed cry or a child sobbing. Everyone started and turned towards him.

Kamilla had stood up. She called the waiter over.

The waiter brought a lantern. Kamilla tidied up her hair. Klara Porges came over to Polzer. 'Are we going home?' she asked.

'If that is your wish, Frau Porges,' replied Polzer.

The head clerk and Herr Fogl each took Kamilla by the arm. They went in front. Then came Frau Porges with the student. The women were talking very loud and laughing. They had drunk a lot of wine. Frau Porges was leaning heavily on the student's arm.

'Where's Polzer got to?' she asked in plaintive tones.

She stopped and only calmed down when Polzer and the doctor appeared.

'So there you are,' she said tenderly and tried to stroke him.

This embarrassed Polzer very much in the presence of the doctor and the student. The other two men were a long way ahead and had not heard.

Polzer walked beside the doctor. He kept his hat pressed firmly over the tear in his trousers.

'Put your hat on, Polzer,' said the doctor. 'The night air is cool.'

Polzer did not reply.

'It's quite dark,' said the doctor.

Polzer stopped in alarm. He tried to see the doctor's face. Did the doctor know?

'Come on,' said the doctor.

After a few steps he added, 'I know you have a hole in your trousers.' He took Polzer's arm.

Polzer felt himself blush bright red. It was dark and the doctor could not see. But in the distance the first lamps had already appeared. Soon they would be in the brightness of the city streets. Polzer pressed his head down on his chest. The gravel crunched under his feet. He hardly dared tread firmly on the ground.

'Herr Polzer,' said the doctor, 'I know I've touched a sore spot. It may seem tactless of me. Put it down to the fact that I'm a doctor and used to feeling painful spots, even taking the knife to them if it's necessary.'

The doctor paused for a moment, then went on, 'I have to admit you haven't asked me to seek out the causes of your pain. I also admit that your astonishment at what I am going to tell you does not seem unreasonable. You hardly know me. But you would be wrong to assume that what I am offering you comes from some deep feeling, from friendship, affection, charity, compassion, humanity or any other of those noble sentiments. I go about it completely without expectations, just as a kind of hobby, so there is no need to feel hurt pride.'

The doctor fell silent again. Polzer could not understand what he was talking about.

'You would be right to reject an act of charity on my part, certainly you would. But you can allow me to indulge a whim. You know that I'm well-off. I don't practise my profession. I travel. Basically, all I've done so far is have a look around. I'm not a compassionate person. I give nothing to the poor. And if I were compassionate, I would certainly not offer you anything, and most certainly not what I am about to offer you. I am offering you this because it corresponds to the image I have of you. I want to make that image a reality. I know nothing about you, but I imagine you come from a good, middle-class family in the provinces. Back home your father will have been a respected merchant, a doctor or a lawyer. I assume your family became impoverished and you, perhaps from having been pampered as a child, lack the energy to achieve a position that would provide you with an income commensurate with your education and upbringing. Is my conjecture correct, Herr Polzer? Or do you have reservations to make?'

In spite of the darkness, Polzer could feel the doctor's questioning look directed at him. He knew that his face was bright red.

'No, no,' he said.

'I can tell that from the decorum with which you manage to wear your old and already rather shabby clothes; from the engaging shyness with which you move inside your suit, well aware of how worn it is. Your whole being exudes the dignity of middle-class tradition. The thing that weighs most heavily on

you, I know, is the fact that your outward appearance is not in harmony with the line of your movements, that it goes against your memories of your
upbringing, your image of your father, I could
almost say. It is a constant burden weighing you
down. That is why you feel inhibited in company
and, I'm sure, in your work as well.'

They had reached the first street lamps. Polzer
pressed his hat firmly against his trousers.

'Now can you guess what I want to suggest?' said
the doctor.

'No,' said Polzer.

'You need a suit. A new, well-cut suit. Shirts and
underwear, hat, shoes, all the things that go with it.
Tomorrow we'll go and select one together, Herr
Polzer. You will regard the cost as a loan, I don't deal
in charity, as you can see. The whole affair will stay
between just the two of us. You know that you can
accept my offer without putting yourself under any
undue obligation to me.'

Polzer looked at him. The doctor smiled and
avoided Polzer's eye. Polzer did not reply.

They went their separate ways at the tram-stop.
Polzer returned home with Frau Porges and only the
student accompanied them. Polzer was thinking of a
long, brown jacket cut away slightly at the front.
Karl Fanta's father had worn a jacket like that. It
was an elegant and dignified article of clothing.

During his lunch hour Polzer went to the tailor's with the doctor. He had been measured up for a brown jacket cut away slightly at the front. That was what Polzer had requested.

When he came back from the bank that evening, he heard Kamilla's voice in the kitchen. He went to his room. Kamilla often came to visit Frau Porges in the evening. On such evenings Franz Polzer would hear the women talking and laughing in the kitchen late into the night.

The sound of the familiar voices from the kitchen made the darkness more bearable. The floorboards did not creak with secret footsteps.

Polzer put his hand up to touch the picture of St. Francis. The last thing he heard was Kamilla's deep laugh before he closed his eyes, reassured.

During the night Polzer suddenly felt he could hear voices beside his bed. First of all farther away and soft, then louder and quite close. Polzer was not asleep, but his eyes were closed tight. He could not raise his eyelids because two thumbs were pressing down on them.

It was strange how clearly Polzer could see everything despite that. He was wearing a brown jacket, slightly cut away at the front, and was quite calm among all the people. He knew that his flies were properly done up and he walked up and down in the spacious rooms, in dignified conversation. Karl was sitting in one corner doing his homework. Polzer was struck by the fact that Karl was naked and that he, Polzer, was not surprised at it. Suddenly, with a horrified start, Polzer felt someone fumbling with his flies. He twisted and turned, shrank back into the dark alcove on the stairs, pushed the hands away, felt yielding flesh under his fingers, tried to touch the picture of St. Francis. He heard laughter and knew that people could see him, tried to shout for help, but his voice failed; he made every effort to form a sound in his throat, but all that came was the hoarse exhalation of his breath. From the dull gleam of the line down the middle, he recognised the parting. He knew that Frau Porges had told everything in order to expose him, to torment him. Why did she hate him? He tried to speak. 'I am the victim,' he tried to say, but his throat was dry, he could not swallow his saliva, however hard he tried. Then the parting fell onto the staircase, together with the head, bounced down the stairs and rolled to a stop in front of the crucifix. The head had suddenly been chopped off. 'Who?' he tried to cry, 'Who?' and beat his breast. They all raised their fingers menacingly and pointed at him. He stood there, helpless, at the mercy of everyone. There was no escape. Now he had to move out, count his things, the underwear was never-ending. There was endless underwear. He had to load it on his back, it kept falling off, because he could not hold it since he had the picture of St. Francis in his hands. Now he was in Žižkov, in a dark room, and his sister was lying there, naked, her breasts slumped down the sides of her body, her legs spread wide. Her body was

moist and shimmering. He knew that her flesh was
soft and dark, and he tried to flee, for there was a
terrible thought inside his head, a thought he could
not bear. The boards creaked under his feet and out
of the door came a man with his nightshirt open. The
man was breathing heavily and raised his fists to hit
Polzer. There was a horrible smell, like fresh rolls.
The picture of St. Francis had gone, but Polzer could
hear laughter beside him and his breath was being
forced back down his throat by the heat of a fat
body, so that he felt he was going to suffocate.

Polzer awoke with a start. He was shaking. He
rubbed his forehead with his hand. The light was on
in his room. Kamilla and Frau Porges were standing
beside his bed.

'What is the time?' asked Franz Polzer in alarm.

'Twelve o'clock,' said Klara Porges. 'You were fast
asleep. Kamilla wanted to ask you how you enjoyed
yesterday. Why did you slip into your room furtively
like that?'

Polzer sat up in bed. He stared at the two women.

'What do you want?' he asked in a toneless voice.

Kamilla came up close to him. 'Herr Polzer, we've
known each other for such a long time. Why are you
giving me that horrified stare?'

She sat down on his bed.

Polzer stretched out his hands to ward her off. 'Oh
God, Frau Porges,' he said, 'what do you want with
me?'

'Be quiet,' said Klara Porges and left the room.

'What must you think of me,' said Kamilla, bending over him. He felt her bosom on his chest. 'Don't

get the wrong idea. I don't want anything from you. Klara's told me everything. Why don't you want Klara? Klara's an attractive woman. She says you don't want her. I'm Klara's friend, Herr Polzer, you can tell me.'

Polzer said nothing. He could see the round tops of her breasts in the opening of her blouse. He closed his eyes and said nothing.

Kamilla was silent too. He felt the warmth of her breath on his cheek. The clock ticked loudly.

Suddenly he felt her hand slowly pushing the bedclothes aside. His mouth opened, but he did not cry out. He heard Kamilla's panting breath.

'Oh, how obedient,' said Kamilla, softly and tenderly, 'doesn't stir at all.'

Why did she tell her? he thought. O God, why did she tell her?

'Doesn't . . . stir . . . at all'

In the hall Klara Porges's footsteps could be heard approaching. Kamilla jumped up. Frau Porges had brought a tot of schnapps for Kamilla. Kamilla offered it to Polzer. Polzer silently refused.

'There's nothing more in the bottle,' said Frau Porges with a laugh.

Polzer heard the apartment door open. Klara Porges was seeing Kamilla out. He heard her steps as she came back. Soon afterwards the bed in the next room creaked. Then there was silence.

Polzer thought of getting up, knocking on Frau Porges's door and asking her why she had done it. Today she had told Kamilla, tomorrow she would tell the head clerk, the student, the doctor. He would have to avoid people, would not be able to leave the apartment, would not be able to go to the bank, for his walk along the river, to the café, to see Karl on Tuesday, tomorrow. Karl would laugh. He could not take her to see Karl. Karl must not hear about it. Karl made fun of him anyway. Karl would burst out laughing. Karl must not see Klara Porges. Where is it all going to end? wondered Polzer. Where is it going to end? Should he tell the doctor, take him into his confidence, then flee? No one would understand all this, not even the doctor would understand it. Polzer would have to ask Frau Porges to take pity on him, beg her for mercy. What had he done? She could not mean him to suffer these torments! He would go and knock at her door. Make an end of it! She would come to him, her nightdress falling, her hair undone, take him by the hand, draw him to her bed, press him to her naked body – no! no! That was the soft, dark flesh, that was the ghastly, incomprehensible memory. No. Better to leave, take another room, that no one knew of, all alone. You never know who is sleeping in the next room. You can hear breathing. Steps crossing the hall. You cannot know everyone in the strange house where you live alone. Perhaps they have keys to the apartment, keys to the cupboards. Perhaps they stand at his door. Listening and waiting until they can hear from his breathing that the occupant is asleep. Even poor people had had attempts made on their lives, because someone thought they had hidden treasure, or out of mindless hatred.

It was completely quiet in Polzer's room. Not even

the floorboards were creaking. Polzer did not dare move.

Something is brewing, thought Polzer.

Something was standing in the dark, waiting. All this had to come to an end. Something was in the corner, waiting. Perhaps a murderer with an axe. You cannot know the house where you live.

Polzer listened. Wasn't that a rustling noise? He could not hear Frau Porges breathing. What was wrong with Frau Porges? Why was Frau Porges not breathing? It was so quiet. What was lurking there? Something was brewing.

.

Frau Porges showed no surprise when Polzer asked her to go to see Karl with him. She seemed to have expected the invitation. On the way there Polzer thought about how to prepare her for everything. But it was only just before they reached the block where Fanta lived that he started to speak.

'He is very ill, Frau Porges,' he said, 'and he is very excitable. He says things that are extremely unusual, Frau Porges, extremely unusual. He is ill, one has to make allowances.'

'We shall see,' said Frau Porges.

'Quite so, Frau Porges, we shall see. He doesn't speak well of his wife, even though she does everything for him. He is an invalid, Frau Porges, one has to let such remarks pass. He has some strange notions. He might even start with one, Frau Porges. One has to let him have his way.'

Frau Porges walked on and did not reply. They were outside the house.

'One more moment, Frau Porges,' said Polzer.

She stopped.

'He might perhaps make a request to you which will surprise you. He is well off, has a fine apartment and a well-run household. But he feels persecuted. He is a sick man, Frau Porges, one must feel sorry for him. I have known him since we were boys. He and his father acted charitably towards me, they deserve my gratitude.'

Frau Porges interrupted him. 'What kind of request?'

'He feels persecuted and wants to move away.'

'To my apartment?'

'To your apartment, Frau Porges.'

Frau Porges thought for a moment. 'We shall see,' she said and set off up the stairs.

Polzer followed her. 'If he should ask to move,' he said quickly, after she had already rung the bell, 'we can't refuse out of hand. He has been visited by misfortune and we must make allowances.'

Dora opened the door. It seemed to Polzer as if she had been standing by the door.

'Delighted to see you,' she said, shaking Frau Porges by the hand. She gave Frau Porges an appraising look. 'Come with me, we'll have a chat together and leave the men to themselves. Come to my room.'

Franz Fanta came out of his room. He greeted Polzer and Klara Porges. Polzer thought he looked paler than usual. His eyes looked tired to Polzer.

Dora had seen Polzer's look. When Franz had gone, she said, 'He's pale and he doesn't look well, does he, Herr Polzer?'

'It's his age,' said Frau Porges.

'But he's so young,' said Dora softly.

'Mature for his years,' replied Klara Porges with a smile. Dora blushed. But Frau Porges went on. Polzer stared at her lips in alarm.

'No need to worry about that. At his age they sleep badly. And God knows what he gets up to, to amuse himself.'

'No, no, Frau Porges,' said Polzer and opened the door to Karl's room.

Karl had heard their voices and was becoming restless.

'Well,' he said, 'where is she? I heard her voice. A clear, calm voice, isn't it? You can tell she's got some flesh on her, not a baby doll like mine. So where is she, Polzer, where is she?'

'She is with Dora.'

'With Dora! Aha, with Dora! She has to be prepared before she can come in. I understand. Clever isn't she, Polzer, my little woman? She'll be telling her not to take anything seriously, I'm ill, so I get these moods. But I'll spoil her little plan, my friend. Have you heard the latest, Polzer? You won't believe it. But first of all tell me, be honest Polzer, am I in my right mind or am I not?'

He gave him a sly look.

'Oh certainly,' said Polzer.

'Oh certainly, oh certainly!' He imitated Polzer's voice. 'Come on now, don't be afraid, give me a straight answer. I won't die of shock, ha, ha, ha.'

'Karl, I beg you . . .'

'No begging, just tell me straight out. Am I in my right mind? Yes or no?'

'Yes.'

At the cost of a great effort, Karl Fanta leant forward. 'Now they're putting it about that I'm mad. They say the illness has started to eat away my brain. She wants to block anything that might happen in advance, to make sure people don't believe me. Move out? The suggestion of a lunatic. Everything I see and hear – are you with me? – just things going on inside my poor, sick imagination. How do I know this? I've suspected it for a long time. Everyone treats me so considerately. They daren't contradict me. They accept everything I say. They all just nod their heads in agreement. You too, oh yes, don't deny it, you too, she's told you I'm mad as well. Shh, don't say anything. I know.

Aren't you afraid of me, Polzer? After all, I'm mad! You believe what she says. Do you think I don't know she went down the stairs with you last time? She poured out her sorrow to you. She had tears in her eyes, the poor unfortunate woman, I know. "My poor husband," she said. Yes, yes,' he laughed and his head wobbled from side to side, 'even if I do spend all day sitting here, I know a lot, more than you people suspect. But after all, I'm just a harmless lunatic, aren't I. I can't move, I can't even lift my hand and smash you in the face because you just sit there, so polite, so considerate, thinking, "We have to let him have his say". You bastard! You bastard!'

Polzer leapt to his feet. 'Sit down!' Karl Fanta screamed. 'I'll call for help.' His fearful eyes were fixed on Franz Polzer. Exhausted, he sank back into his chair.

Polzer had quickly sat down again. He shifted uneasily in his chair. 'But Karl . . .' he said timidly.

'You can soft-soap me as much as you like, my lad, I know I'm in my right mind. I see what I see and I hear what I hear. When you can't get around yourself, you need your informers. And there's no shortage of them, thank God! You don't go mad, my son.

Au contraire! Your wits get razor-sharp, your mind's as clear as can be. I can still hear things when the rest of you think it's silent as the grave. I know I'm in my right mind, and you can go ahead and tell darling Dora that. Tell her everything I've told you. That I'm going to thwart her plans, Polzer, that I know how to deal with that poor child and all her suffering. It's really terrible, you're thinking, this man demanding such awful things of her. Oh yes, I'm all sweetness and light when I talk to her, but I have to have my little performance. What d'you think would happen if I were to shout and scream, Polzer? She'd laugh me out of court! But when I wheedle and cajole? No, no, whether Dora's still my darling little girl or not, she doesn't laugh at me, but does my bidding as obediently as a girl picked up off the streets. She does cry, but only when she's alone. And she's afraid of me and wonders how she can get away from me.'

'Dora doesn't want to get away from you,' said Polzer. 'She wants to do everything you demand. She wants to do it herself, without a nurse. Dora's unhappy that you want to leave.'

'Aha, so that's what she told you, did she? Polzer, Polzer! I know you're not one of the brightest. God, I don't mean to hurt you. You may perhaps have come to see it yourself. At school even, and then afterwards? You just happen to be rather limited. You don't mind my saying so, do you? I'll be honest with you: you're a petty bank clerk and that's about it as far as you're concerned. Maybe you realise that yourself, hm?'

'Yes,' said Franz Polzer softly.

'Then at least you can listen to me, Polzer! She doesn't want a male nurse, you say? Because she loves me? Because the stench from my sores doesn't nauseate her? Because she's my wife and doesn't want someone else to come between her and me? Ha! Ha! Is that what she said? You see how clear-headed I am? Well, I can tell you there've already been other males coming between her and me. She doesn't want a nurse so that I will continue to be an object she can push around as she likes, nothing more. As soon as I have a male nurse, I'll have a will of my own. I'll get him to push me here, there. I'll send him to the door to see who's come, give him letters to post. He will be my ears, my eyes, my tongue and my legs. Do you understand now, Polzer? Has the penny finally dropped? And she won't let me leave? Because she loves me so much, because she couldn't bear life without me, would die of longing? The poor, darling child? Don't you believe it, Polzer! There are two things at stake. Shall I tell you what they are? But of course you believe I'm mad.'

'How can you think that, Karl?'

'All right then, I'll tell you. But pull your chair closer, Polzer, right up beside me. Walls have ears. Recently I have begun to notice that the boy is taking her side too. Well, let him! He has my face, people say. But the way he looks is not from me. He got that from his mother. I'm convinced he was listening at the door once. He gives me funny looks. He comes in and goes straight out again. Well that's all right by me, Polzer. But I was going to tell you why my little baby doll would die of longing. First of all because of other people. She sets great store by other people. And they'd be surprised, shake their heads and talk. They'd say she wasn't doing the right thing. She has a bad conscience. But that's not the important thing. I'll tell you what the important thing is. I spoke to her once. "Dora darling, my little dove," I said. The words just came into my head. "My little dove," I said, "what a terrible life you have. You're young, and still beautiful, even if your figure's never been the same since giving birth. Your stomach muscles've gone all slack. But no one sees that when you've got your clothes on. And you have to live with me. I'm not a man any more – no, Dora, my little angel, don't say anything, I'm well aware of it. And I often think," I said, "that it would be my duty to release you. Leave the apartment, get a divorce so you can find another husband who would play other games with you than I can play. What kind of game is that for a young woman, to have her breasts stroked?! A child's game, really. Perhaps I can find another woman for whom that pleasure would be sufficient. An older woman with strong nerves who would put up with my illness in return for my money. She doesn't have to be beautiful, she doesn't have to be young, I don't need that any more, haha. Perhaps I'd like an ugly one even better, really, I almost find beauty boring, yes, a woman with two big, fat, sagging breasts!"

She gave me a horrified look. Now I knew the truth. "You needn't worry," I said. "You know best of all how much I love you, Dora, my little dove.

You'll be provided for. You know what's in my will, Dora darling."

"Oh Karl," she said, bursting into tears, "oh Karl,"

I stayed silent for a while, as if I were thinking hard. Then I said slowly, "I have not the slightest intention of changing my will in any way. On top of that, you have certain rights guaranteed by law."

At that she stopped crying and gave me a searching look. Do you see now what it's all about? We don't talk about it any more, but she's thinking about my will. As long as I'm here, I can't change it without her knowing. She's worried about the money. She thinks if I leave, I'll get a divorce. She's not forgotten one word of that conversation. Haha, now even you can understand what it's all about! That's why she's afraid of your widow. She's shut herself up with her to prepare her, d'you understand? But I'm just as clever as she is. It won't do her any good, my friend.

So now you see, Polzer. It's all about money, about money and not the little quirks of a sick man. She'll fight with any weapon that comes to hand, fight, that is, until I am dead and she inherits, and nothing can take the money away from her. God grant it may be soon, she's thinking. And if it shows no sign of happening, what is there to stop her giving a helping hand? Who would be surprised if I'm found dead one day? People are more surprised at the opposite.

But where are they, Polzer? I think they've had enough time. Where is your widow? If she's as fat as you say, then I imagine her breasts will sag, won't

they, even though she hasn't had any children? Oh
dear, what have I said? What delicate feelings have I
trampled on? Aah,' said Karl Fanta, in the tone in
which women talk to little children, 'now the poor
little thing's blushing. How old is he then, what's the
matter with him, then? Off you go, Polzer, and see
what your widow's doing.'

Klara Porges was sitting in Dora's room. Dora had
drawn a comfortable chair over to the window for her.
Frau Porges looked round and scrutinised the furnishings. On the tables were fine lace cloths and
valuable porcelain figures.

'Wouldn't you like to take your jacket off?' asked
Dora.

Frau Porges sensed the faint odour of a perfume
spray. 'No,' she said curtly.

Dora, who had stood up to help her off with her
jacket, drew back. She gave Frau Porges a questioning look.

She wants something from me, Frau Porges
thought. She saw some resemblance to Franz Fanta
in Dora's features. Why had Franz Fanta not come in
with them? Was he ashamed of her in his mother's
presence?

'You don't trust me?' Dora asked softly.

'Don't trust?' Frau Porges shrugged her shoulders
and made a dismissive gesture. 'I'm looking at the
room. You have very beautiful furnishings. This lace
and the porcelain. Not long ago a woman I know
paid three hundred crowns for a figure like that. And
it had a fault. I presume these are perfect.'

Dora looked down and said nothing.

'You have lovely perfume, Frau Fanta. I don't use perfume. You can never cover up the smell of washing. You can't get rid of it. It's nice to be rich, haha.'

The trimming on Dora's slip was visible in the opening of her house-dress.

'A slip like that, for example. No, no! Doesn't it get torn in the wash? You must have a lover to wear such fine lingerie. You can tell me, Frau Fanta.'

'Oh, God,' said Dora, 'how can you think such a thing! If you knew what I have to go through you wouldn't talk to me like that, Frau Porges, no, I'm sure you wouldn't.' She put her head in her hands and sobbed.

Frau Porges stood up and went over to her. 'God, now you're crying, Frau Fanta. I really didn't mean to hurt you. Wealth isn't everything, I know that. Don't cry like that, Frau Fanta.'

'I know you don't mean any harm,' said Dora tearfully, 'I know that, Frau Porges. Oh, if you only knew . . . no one to talk to, no one to pour out my heart to. Only Polzer. Polzer's the only one. He's a good man, isn't he?'

'Yes, yes, only stop crying.'

'You love Polzer, don't you Frau Porges? Go on, tell me.'

'Well . . .' said Frau Porges.

'No, no, please trust me. Tell me.'

'He needs special handling,' said Klara Porges.

'He's the only one I can tell everything, Frau Porges. He's good to me. If you only knew what I have to go through, how I am tormented. No, I just couldn't tell you, ever. I would die of shame.'

She started to cry again.

Frau Porges put her hand on her shoulder.

Dora grasped Frau Porges's hand.

'Will you help me, Frau Porges? He asked to see you. He'll like you, Frau Porges.'

'Like me?'

'Yes, yes. I don't please him any more, even though I do everything he asks. Oh, if you only knew, Frau Porges. There's not another woman would do those things. But he wants women with some flesh on them, he says. I'm too delicate, he says.' She squeezed Klara Porges's hand. 'Will you help me?' she asked.

'We shall see,' said Klara Porges.

'Oh thank you,' said Dora, bending down to kiss Frau Porges's hand. The widow quickly pulled it away. She had gone red in the face.

'What are you doing?' she said. 'You shouldn't be doing that, a lady like you! You're overwrought, Frau Fanta.'

'No, no, you're so good to me. I didn't dare hope, Frau Porges. He will try to use you against me. He wants to have a male nurse. Did you know that? It mustn't happen, Frau Porges. He'd torment me even more once he didn't need me. He'd tell people I refused to go on dressing his sores, that's why he has to have a nurse. He wants to leave me, go right away. Had you heard that, Frau Porges? He says he wants to move in with Polzer. That's why he wants to meet you. Frau Porges, you must help me. He says I have lovers and that's why he has to get out of the house.'

'And what do you want?'

'He must stay, Frau Porges, don't you understand.
I do everything he asks. I want him to stay.'

'You haven't got a lover?'

'How can you think that, Frau Porges? No, no!'

'You ought to have one. You're a beautiful woman.
How can you bear it, Frau Fanta? You'll see everything differently if you have a lover. I'm sure that
really he knows you haven't got one, that's why he
torments you like this. If he knew you had someone
else, he'd pretend he knew nothing about it. After all,
he's a cripple, not a man any longer.'

'Don't say things like that, Frau Porges, please,'
Dora pleaded. 'Tell me what's to be done.'

'What's to be done? Well get a nurse first of all!
Why ever don't you want one?'

'But I told you, Frau Porges. He'll shut me out
completely if I get one. He won't need me any longer
and won't have to take me into consideration at all.
And what will people say? And Franz? No, no, I'd be
ashamed to face my own child. Please help me, Frau
Porges, I beg you, I beseech you. It can't be allowed
to happen.'

'I don't understand you,' said Frau Porges. 'I
don't understand all this fuss. It'll be easier for you if
he has a nurse. You're rich. Why dress his sores yourself? It's an odd thing to do. If I were rich I'd take
on, what? two nurses. Porges was very ill as well.
What I went through with him! You wouldn't believe
it. Real worries. I looked after Porges, and you can
have no idea what that means when the money's
short. If I'd had the money, I wouldn't have thought

about it for a second.' She took a deep breath. 'But I shouldn't go on about Porges, it just makes me sad. He didn't have an easy time of it, and nor did I. He left me here, helpless, poor, without friends.' She dabbed her eyes with her handkerchief. 'Just look at the apartment you've got. All this fuss just because your husband wants to have a nurse? As for moving out, that can wait. Once he's got his nurse, perhaps he'll be satisfied. You really haven't got anything to worry about.'

'What should I do, Frau Porges?'

'First of all you must let him have his nurse. You have to think of yourself. It's getting too much for you. Everything will be better, you'll see. Just think it over.'

'Perhaps you're right.' Dora dried her eyes. 'I will think it over. It might well turn out to be less difficult than I thought.'

Franz Polzer came in. 'He's asking for you,' he said.

Karl sat up in his chair, as far as he was able. He scrutinised Frau Porges.

'You're surprised, now, aren't you,' he said. 'This isn't quite what you imagined, is it? Do sit down. Not too close, I stink somewhat. That chair's reserved for my little girl. Come on, Dora darling, sit here by my side. That's it. I can't shake hands with you, either, Frau Porges. Mine are too damp, my palms sweat a lot. Just so you know and can take appropriate precautions, haha! Dry my hands, darling,' he said, turning to Dora. 'So, you know

everything now, I presume? It took long enough.
Dora has told you everything, yes? Prepared you
properly for what you were going to see? She's too
good is my Dora. I'm a lucky man to have found a
wife like that. She prepares my visitors so that I'm
not hurt by the expressions on their faces. You did
tell her everything, didn't you, my dear? Is there
anything left for me to tell? Well, I wouldn't be surprised if you kept quiet about how good to me you
are, how big a debt of gratitude I owe you because
you fulfil my every wish. A cripple has some funny
ideas, you know. You're not a man any more and yet
sometimes you get the urge. Did she tell you that,
Frau Porges?'

'Karl!' said Dora.

'"Karl! Karl!" What's troubling my little angel?'

'Your wife told me nothing,' said Klara Porges.
'She showed me the furniture and the washing.'

'The washing! D'you hear, Polzer, the washing!
Who would have thought it? But it's very plausible.
What do women do in this kind of situation? If you
think about it carefully, there's only one conclusion.
They look at the furniture and the washing. I bet
there was the odd dirty item in the washing, wasn't
there? Not surprising, really when you consider my
illness. I can't feel my stools coming. You have to
guess when it might be necessary, and often you
guess wrong. There was a time when I wasn't like
this. Just think, Frau Porges, this piece of shit you
see before you used to be a handsome man! Did she
tell you that while she was showing you the washing?
Not stupid, but kind-hearted and cheerful. Nothing

but good qualities. *De mortuis nil nisi bene.* Translate it, Polzer, go on, translate it.'

'Say nothing but good of the dead,' said Polzer.

'"Of the dead," that refers to me. Does a lovely funeral oration, does Polzer. And so tactful, too, Frau Porges, so tactful! You can consider yourself lucky to have found such a companion. But dear old Polzer's hit the jackpot too, hasn't he, Dora darling? Who would have thought he had it in him?! Beautiful, isn't she, my angel? Don't I keep telling you: a full figure! Just look at her, just look at her!'

'Please, Herr Fanta,' said Frau Porges, 'you're embarrassing me.'

'Am I? No, no, I didn't mean to, Frau Porges. I was just saying what I thought. But why bother? You're right. I have more important things to talk about, Frau Porges, to talk about with you. You see, my little Dora's so busy taking care of me she hasn't got the time. And then she lacks the necessary experience. What I wanted to ask you ... We've agreed, Dora and I – did she have time to tell you? – that I should have a male nurse. She can't continue to put up with this heavy load. She took it on out of her love for me, and she's unhappy with the idea of giving it up, but she realises it's necessary and has agreed.'

Dora was about to say something, but Frau Porges got in first. 'Your wife did tell me, Herr Fanta, and she asked for my assistance in this matter.'

Dora looked at Frau Porges, but said nothing.

'Well, then,' said Karl Fanta.

'Well, then,' said Klara Porges, 'I've already

thought the matter over. It has to be a man who's reliable. And you're heavy, Herr Fanta, so he has to be strong. I'll discuss it with Kamilla. Yes, Kamilla, she's a friend of mine. We'll look out for a strong, sturdy man, Herr Fanta, a stocky man. Don't let yourself be misled, stocky men are more powerful than tall ones. Height isn't the important thing. That's what'll be best.'

'Agreed,' said Karl Fanta. 'I'm delighted you're willing to help like this. You'll soon be free now, my little dove. Lean your face down, I feel a longing to stroke your cheek.'

Dora bent down towards him. Her face was bright red. Polzer turned away and looked out of the window.

'Look,' said Karl Fanta, 'my hands are soaking, but it doesn't bother Dora. Look, Frau Porges.'

Frau Porges stood up. Dora accompanied her to the door. Polzer noticed Karl beckoning him over with his head. He went up close to Karl's chair.

'She's got the smell, too,' Karl Fanta whispered. 'Have you noticed it? A remarkable smell, a slight smell of sweat. I bet she sweats under her armpits, eh Polzer? Have a look and tell me.' He leant back. 'Just the way I thought it would be, Polzer, just the way I thought.'

On the day his new suit was due to be finished, the doctor met Polzer from work. They went to a shirt-maker's, where the doctor bought him three shirts, collars and a tie.

Polzer went along with everything. Several times he tried to say something, but the doctor cut him short. Finally Polzer managed at least to indicate to the doctor that he by no means regarded these expenses as a present. He had, he said, thought it over.

'I will pay everything back,' he went on. 'I hope –' he found it difficult to talk about it, '– you will have no objection to being repaid in instalments. I intend to make a payment on the first of every month.'

The doctor made a dismissive gesture. 'Let's go to the shoemaker's now.'

Polzer chose patent-leather shoes. He compared their shine with the shine on the shoes he polished himself and realised how incomparably more beautiful was the reflection of the light in his patent-leather shoes. They gave him a chamois cloth, with which he immediately removed a few specks of dust from his new shoes.

They also bought a hat. It was a black felt hat. Then they went to the tailor's. There Polzer put his new clothes on. He blushed when he looked in the mirror. The suit draped itself smoothly and closely round Polzer's body. He turned away from the mirror quickly and did not dare look at the doctor and the tailor, fearing there would be a smile on their lips. He had recognised the slightly cut-away, long brown jacket. Surely everyone would see he was wearing another man's jacket? It had just been a vague image in his mind and now he was horrified at the extreme similarity. In embarrassment Polzer let his hands drop to his sides. He had been holding them clasped behind his back and remembered that had been the usual posture of Karl's father.

Polzer did not dare look up. He muttered a few words of thanks and hurried home. He hoped the doctor, who had not known Karl Fanta's father, would not notice anything. He couldn't visit Karl in this outfit. Karl would be certain to recognise it at once and expose Polzer's imposture.

Klara Porges refused to believe the doctor had bought everything, until Polzer had repeated it several times. She admired every item, was astonished to see that the jacket was lined with silk and praised the quality linen of the shirts.

'Polzer,' she said, 'you look like a real gentleman.'

Without looking at her, Polzer said, 'it's just a simple suit, Frau Porges. I'm paying the doctor back in monthly instalments.'

'Those shoes!' said Frau Porges. 'you can see yourself in them like a mirror.'

'Patent leather,' said Polzer, 'is not guaranteed.'

'They should only be worn in fine weather.'

'You have to tread carefully in them, Frau Porges,' said Polzer, 'and take care that no one steps on them.

You clean them with this chamois leather, after first breathing on the patent leather.'

'Oh Polzer,' said Frau Porges. 'If only you loved me just a little bit, Polzer.' She took his hand. 'We could be so happy,' she said, giving way to emotion.

Polzer knew what was coming. He bent down to take off his patent-leather shoes and wrap them up in a cloth. They had to be protected from dust. He could feel Frau Porges looking at him. She had overcome her outburst of emotion.

She gave a silent laugh and came up to him. The torment to come was familiar from many nights. She pushed him down onto the floor and grabbed him. Why would she not leave him alone, why would she not forgive him? He wanted to tell her about the thought he could not get out of his mind. She would often let go of him, while he was lying on the floor, order him to stand up and finish it off with his own hands in front of her. She lay back on the pillows, naked, her lips twisted in a laugh. Her body was spread out, her ample flesh brazenly spilling over the whole bed. Polzer closed his eyes. He heard her shouted command dictating the speed, and obeyed. Sometimes she leapt up and enfolded him in her arms. She dragged him down, forcing him into contact with her bloated flesh. He felt the dampness of her skin and smelt her smell. It was a faint smell of soap. It was a smell Karl could not recognise. Polzer could. Her parting was right in front of his eyes. He recognised the parting, too. There was a thought inside him, immense and terrible, which he could not understand and could not overcome. He wanted to

ask the widow to comb out her parting, but he did
not dare. He thought everything would be easier if
she combed out her parting. Then that thought
would be no more, that sinful, blasphemous thought
that he was having intercourse with the sister who
had never existed. St. Francis ought to come down
from the wall to go into Frau Porges's room with him
in order to protect him. The Jews do not love the
saints. Even Karl, when they were still boys, had
had a horror of the crucifix on their dark staircase.
Frau Porges would not let the saint in. With her
Polzer was not under the protection of the saint.
He resolved to light a candle to him now and then,
secretly. No one was to know about it.

Polzer had reddish hair on his chest like his father,
who had felt women's constantly moving breasts.
Polzer had seen his father's hair under his nightshirt.
Tufts of red mixed with grey. All those years ago,
when his father had come out of the widow's, sister's,
aunt's room. Even a sister has breasts that are constantly moving and a woman's open flesh. Klara
Porges was not a sister, she did not belong to the
family. Porges was dead. What was her flesh to
Polzer? Polzer did not want her soft widow's flesh
that felt warm and was covered in dark down. Why
did she make him suffer this torment? Why did she
keep grabbing him and why would she not forgive
him?

He did not leave her room until it was light. He
would sit on a chair or on the floor in a corner of the
room. Frau Porges slept. He heard her loud breathing. Polzer knew that in the darkness of the hall,

which he had to cross, and in his own room the mystery was even more impenetrable and menacing than here, protected by the presence of Frau Porges. Polzer did not move, so as not to wake her. She lay there with her mouth open and did not hear him when he quietly left the room in the morning.

In the bank Polzer's suit caused a stir. Young Wodak stared at Polzer, speechless. Only when Polzer had sat down at his desk as usual did he recover his composure.

'Herr Polzer,' he said, 'you're wearing a new suit!'

Polzer said nothing. Wodak came over to him. 'And patent-leather shoes! What's happened, Herr Polzer?'

Since Polzer did not answer, Wodak went on. 'Is it perhaps because you're angry with me, Herr Polzer? I may have offended you once, Herr Polzer, but I didn't mean to, believe me. I won't do it again, I promise. But don't look at me like that, say something, please. At least tell me you're not angry with me.'

'No, no, Herr Wodak,' said Polzer, 'I'm not angry with you. You haven't done anything to offend me. You're a good man, I know that, Herr Wodak.'

'Thank you.' Wodak shook his hand. 'It's wonderful cloth, Herr Polzer. And lined throughout with silk! But the cut's a little unusual, don't you think? Like in old pictures?'

Polzer started. Did Wodak know something? He gave the young man a searching look.

'I'm sure you gave the instructions yourself. It shows you have taste. You don't want the latest fashion. That demonstrates true refinement, Herr Polzer, really. And it looks perfect on you.'

Polzer had started working. Young Wodak watched him. Several times he started to ask a question. Then Wodak left the room. He hurried with his news to the large accounts office. People clustered round him. Some wanted to rush off to Polzer, to see his suit. Herr Fogl held them back.

'That would be tactless,' he said, 'tactless in the extreme. We'll all see him, gentlemen, but let's wait till the opportunity arises. Herr Polzer didn't say anything about how he came by this new suit? Patent-leather shoes, you say, Herr Wodak, a new tie, eh? All tip-top quality?'

'All tip-top quality, Herr Fogl. He must have come into an inheritance, or had a win on the lottery. A big win! Anyone who knows him would be in no doubt about that. I've been sitting opposite him for three years now, I know what I'm talking about. He'd starve rather than spend one copper unnecessarily.'

'Have you noticed any change in him recently, Herr Wodak?'

'A few things. He seems to be keyed up all the time. And I'm pretty sure he must have bought a lottery ticket. I remember I once found the list of winning numbers on his desk.

'It's clear,' said Herr Fogl, 'that our colleague has either had a big win or come into an inheritance. I suggest, gentlemen, we appoint two delegates to present Herr Polzer with heartiest congratulations on the part of his fellow employees.'

Fogl and Wodak were elected and immediately went to Polzer. Fogl took up position before him in a dignified posture.

'Esteemed colleague,' he said, with solemn cere-
mony, 'I appear before you, together with our
colleague Wodak, as a representative of the staff of
the Accounts Department to transmit to you the
congratulations of your immediate colleagues.'

Polzer gazed at the two in bewilderment. Their
posture as well as the solemn tone of the speech
completely baffled him. He felt two pairs of eyes
resting earnestly on him and stood up.

He realised that Fogl was congratulating him, but
could not understand all the words that came from
Fogl's lips. All he knew was that he must correct him,
tell him that none of it was true, that they had got it
wrong about the suit, that he had neither had a win
on the lottery nor come into an inheritance. Fogl
called him a model of devotion to duty, extolled him
with expressions at which Polzer ought to have
demurred. Now Fogl's voice was quivering with suppressed emotion. He concluded his speech. He shook
Polzer by the hand. The tears had crept into Polzer's
eyes.

'I thank you,' he said, 'I thank you. You are very
kind to me, but . . . I thank you.'

Fogl and Wodak withdrew quickly. They did not
want to witness Polzer succumbing to emotion.

The next day Polzer was called to see the manager.
The manager scrutinised Polzer for a moment, then
invited him to sit down.

'You've been at the bank for sixteen years,' said
the manager, leaning back in his chair.

'Seventeen years, Herr Direktor,' said Polzer.

'By all reports your work is excellent. And your

118

position is one where you could be replaced by someone less valuable. Our best employees are more urgently needed elsewhere. Have you any particular wish?'

Polzer shook his head.

'Well then,' said the manager, 'if you're agreeable, from the first of next month you'll be transferred to the Commodities Department. You'll be under Herr König.'

The manager stood up and shook his hand. At the door Polzer turned round to tell the manager that his wish was to stay where he was, that it would be difficult to hand over his work to someone else, someone who was not used to it. He wanted to explain everything, that the suit was a present from the doctor, that he had not come into an inheritance, that he had not had a win on the lottery, that he had not been able to get a word in and that was the cause of the misunderstanding. He wanted to admit everything.

The manager was already signing letters in a file on the table in front of him and not looking at Polzer any more.

The Commodities Department was one floor lower down. There were ten days to go until the move. Polzer was seized with agitation. Not everything could be done in ten days. He had to instruct the new clerk in his duties. The young man appeared the very next day. He sat beside Polzer and watched him while he worked. The desk at which he had worked until now was to stay upstairs. The drawers were full of old papers, letters, forms. All these would have to be transferred. That could only be done on the evening of the tenth day. Until then they had to stay up there. Another problem was that the key to his new desk could not be found. A new key had to be made, which meant fetching a locksmith. Polzer would have to do it himself, if he wanted a craftsman he could rely on. He would have to ask Frau Porges where there was a locksmith and go and see him during one of his lunch breaks. And it was doubtful whether the key could be made in a few days. If the locksmith did not deliver it on time, the drawers of his new desk would be open to unauthorised persons. He would be unable to stop things disappearing, indeed, it would be impossible to be absolutely certain whether something had disappeared or not. Nothing could stop the unease caused by this uncertainty growing to terrifying proportions. To be exposed to surreptitious theft with no means of telling whether one had actually occurred was to be left defenceless.

The was a telephone on the desk on the floor below. His new position demanded frequent telephone conversations. You might mishear and come to the wrong conclusion, or forget something you had correctly understood. You could not take your eye off the handset, any moment it might start ringing in its shrill tones, you were on tenterhooks, in constant apprehension of the sudden event that could assail you at any time and from any direction, tearing you out of your ordered activity. Even if your bodily needs required it, you would not dare to leave the room. You had to be ready, he was told, to reply to enquiries unprepared, to give out binding information, you had to expect new developments which would change your plan of work. It would be farewell to calm, to order. You had to talk, make decisions, be quick, be able to cope. You might get things wrong, mix things up in haste, be careless, make mistakes for which you had to bear the responsibility. You would have no time. The tasks could not be completed in a day, unfinished business would pile up on your desk, there was unrest all around, people came, brought files, asked questions, everything piled up, became disordered. Polzer would get stuck, the jumbled heap of papers was too great, everything was in chaos. The thought of the dangerous insecurity of having to be prepared for a thousand unexpected, unforeseeable eventualities kept him awake at nights. He was afraid of the haste in which everything had to be done. Everyone around was looking at him, putting pressure on him. Speed was demanded. What was done was being done too slowly. You could not take sufficient care, be precise, deal with things in their proper order, files on this side, files on that side, the telephone, people, chaos, you had no time. The secretary came for dictation. He had to dictate his correspondence to her fluently. That required experience and practice. Polzer had neither. Full of apprehension, he realised he would get stuck in the middle of sentences, not knowing how to go on, and feel ashamed in front of the secretary. The typists would snigger at him. Very quickly it was bound to become obvious that he was not up to it, that they had overestimated his abilities.

Then there would be nothing left for it but to return to his old place, shamed, his status undermined.

They all behaved with great politeness towards Polzer. People greeted him first. Every morning Wodak enquired after his health. His new boss offered him a cigar. Polzer declined with thanks, informing him that he only smoked on special occasions. What he wanted to say was that he had not had a win on the lottery and that he did not deserve all this politeness. He worked out an explanation for his new suit. He decided to tell people that for years he had been saving up his coppers for this very purpose. To admit that he had accepted it as a present from the doctor would have made him the laughing-stock of the bank. That was a shame he could not reveal. He had to wrap it up in a lie and keep the guilt hidden inside him for ever. Several times he tried to bring the conversation round to this, but his colleagues refused to go along with it. They took his hints as excuses and received them with understanding smiles. Polzer realised that they did not want to listen to him.

A couple of days before Polzer was due to take up his new position, he was invited to visit Karl Fanta with Frau Porges. Polzer wore his old suit. The drawing-room was brightly lit, the lid of the grand piano open. Kamilla was there too. Together with Klara she had found a male nurse and brought him to the apartment a few days previously.

Karl was sitting in his wheelchair in one corner. Behind him was his nurse. Franz Polzer went up to Karl.

'This is Herr Sonntag,' said Karl, 'my new nurse. I'm very happy with him.'

Franz Polzer shook hands with him.

'You can go now,' said Karl, 'I don't need you.'

The nurse bowed. At the door he stopped beside Kamilla and Frau Porges. Then he left.

'I can't talk to anyone without a witness,' said Karl. 'He's always standing behind me, mute and immobile. If I ask him something, he just answers with a yes or no. Do you think he's secretly in league with Dora?'

'He makes a good impression,' said Polzer. 'Knows his place.'

'What a judge of character!' said Karl. 'It was high time he came. My left arm! It's going to be operated on pretty soon. The doctor has already dropped some hints. That'll probably be the beginning of the end ... No, no, don't feel you have to contradict me, don't feel you have to contradict me.'

The women joined them.

'Are you happy with Sonntag?' Kamilla asked. 'He's powerfully built. That's very important if he's to carry you.'

'He's very useful,' said Karl. 'He just grasps me round the trunk and picks me up like a child. Now I don't need to bother darling Dora any more. He's also very good at dressing my sores. I thank you, ladies, for going to such trouble in choosing a nurse for me. Have you thanked these ladies, Dora dear? It's all for your sake, my child.'

'The man looks good,' said Frau Porges. 'He used to be a butcher.'

'Haha!' Karl gave a laugh. 'A butcher! That I
didn't know! That's excellent. He'll soon have work
to do, your butcher. My left arm's due to go under the
knife. Did my little Dora tell you? It may be different
from slaughtering calves, but his experience with
calves should still stand him in good stead. He won't
turn a hair. He'll be a comfort for little Dora, don't
you think, a support?'

Another guest came, a tenor from the opera. He
kissed the women's hands. Frau Porges blushed and
tried to pull her hand away.

The singer often came to visit the Fantas. He sang
and Frau Dora accompanied him.

'Maestro!' cried Karl. 'The darling of the ladies!
You must tell me what you've been up to during the
last few weeks, you Don Juan, you! You look well,
despite all that. I think you've put on a little weight
again since I last saw you. It's love that makes you
fat, maestro, didn't you know that? Our ladies will
always leave the front door open for a tenor, haha. I
know that from my darling Dora. She tells me about
your successes. I think the poor girl must dream of
you, maestro. You should take pity on her. She's dry-
ing up here with me, just look at her, not an ounce of
spare flesh left on her.'

The singer gave an embarrassed smile. He wiped
the sweat from his brow with a silk handkerchief and
turned to the ladies.

'She invites him every week,' said Karl. 'She's fat-
tening him up at my expense, the swine. She invited
him today so I can't talk to your widow. He stinks of
Cologne like a hairdresser. It makes me want to spew,

but the women like it. Just see how they look at him.
What they'd most like to do is just go and undo his
trousers. Observe him carefully. Do you think he goes
to bed with Dora? Observe him carefully.'

'You shouldn't think such things of her.'

'Fool! I bet you think you're the only one who has
your Klara Porges. She doesn't look as if she'd be
satisfied with just you, locust that she is! That idiot's
pulling out all the stops with her. I think it'll all be
settled by tomorrow, Polzer. It doesn't look as if she's
about to say no. She's probably had her fill of skin
and bones. Over here, maestro,' Karl shouted, 'Leave
the women, come and tell me all about it.'

The tenor pulled up a chair.

'Well?' asked Karl. 'Don't keep us waiting. Fat or
thin?'

'Thin,' said the singer in a low voice.

'I know all about that,' said Karl. Dora and the
two women were going to go to another room. 'Stay
with us, Dora dear. There's no need to be embarrassed, my little innocent. You should at least hear
something of what's going on. You'll forget everything, stuck here with me, poor thing. How was it
then, maestro, come on, tell us.'

The tenor whispered something to Karl.

'Oh, Dora darling,' Karl cried, 'pity you didn't
hear. Three times, you say? No wonder women run
after you! What do you say to that, Dora dear? She's
thin and black-haired, you say? I can see her as if she
were here in front of me. Breasts just big enough to
sit in the palm of your hand. Dora dear, it could
almost be you he's talking about. Just be careful,

children, just be careful. We don't want any disasters, do we? You understand what I'm saying?'

'What a way to talk is that?' said Frau Porges.

Dora looked helplessly at Polzer. Polzer wanted to say something, but Karl gave him an angry look.

'You must have a go with a fat one some time,' said Karl. 'You soon get bored with thin ones, believe me. You feel like getting your hands on something a bit more substantial for once. Isn't that so, Polzer?'

The tenor stood up. 'Would you accompany me, Frau Fanta?' he asked.

Dora went to the piano.

Meanwhile tea was brought in.

The nurse held Karl Fanta's cup for him. His teacup in one hand, a piece of cake in the other, Franz Polzer was sitting directly opposite the singer, who had started singing. The tenor's broad thorax swelled.

'Look at his big mouth,' said Karl in a low voice to Polzer. 'How can a man sing? A woman singing, yes. But a man?! Pampers his windpipe, strikes a pose and opens his big mouth. It's unnatural!'

'I almost think myself,' said Polzer, 'that singing is an undignified occupation for a man.'

'You almost think so yourself, do you, Polzer? Well that's fine, then.'

It seemed to Polzer the singer had heard their conversation. The singer was looking at Polzer, who did not dare to raise his eyes. Polzer went bright red. In consternation he suddenly felt the singer's gaze was fixed on his red hands, which were holding his teacup and piece of cake. With a horrified start he tried to hide those terrible hands as quickly as possible. His cup fell on the floor.

The singer broke off singing. Everyone gathered round Polzer. Polzer stood up.

'What is it?' asked Kamilla. 'What's the matter with you, Herr Polzer?'

'He's clumsy,' said Klara Porges, giving Polzer an angry look. 'You must forgive him.'

'It's nothing,' said Dora. 'Calm down, Herr Polzer.'

Karl Fanta's nurse picked up the pieces.

'Sit down,' said Karl in a low voice. 'At least the singing's stopped.'

Flustered, Polzer say down.

Kamilla handed the tenor a glass of water. Dora rang for the maid. Frau Porges set about helping the nurse. Polzer was the cause of all this fuss going on round him while he sat helplessly next to Karl.

'Forgive me,' he said to Karl, 'forgive me. My hand started trembling.' He knew he had to keep talking. No one said anything. He was the child that had soiled the room. People were angry with him because he was old enough to know better. He went on speaking to Karl. 'I'm being transferred to a different department,' he said. 'The day after tomorrow. But that's impossible. Things need to be kept in order . . . done it for years . . . everything in order. Not a jot, not a tittle out of place. Who knows what will happen when the new clerk does it. A young man. Everything might get muddled up.'

Karl was not listening. He was watching Frau Porges bending down beside the nurse and mopping up the damp carpet with a cloth. Karl could see down her blouse.

The next day Franz Polzer went to see the manager. He had not yet ordered the replacement key. The drawer in the desk on the floor below could still not be locked. That evening he would have to move his things.

The bank manager looked up, questioning.

'I have a request, Herr Direktor,' said Polzer, then faltered.

'Yes, Herr Polzer?' said the manager.

'Everything's in perfect order, Herr Direktor, for handing over,' said Polzer. 'Not a jot anywhere, for years, Herr Direktor . . . but if the young man who is to take over my desk, Herr Direktor . . . I can't keep an eye on it from downstairs . . . everything might get muddled up . . .'

He realised he had become confused and broke off. The manager was chewing a cigar and looking at him in silence. Polzer grew uneasy. The manager might lose his patience. Polzer had to say it quickly.

'I must stay,' he said. 'I mean it would be better if I stayed, to keep things in order, Herr Direktor. After all, seventeen years with neither a jot or a tittle . . . and now everything might get muddled up.'

The bank manager did not reply.

'And downstairs the drawer is unlocked,' said Polzer. Why did the manager stay silent? He might end up using the opportunity to give him the sack. Take away his livelihood. He probably wasn't efficient enough. Yes, that was it. The others worked more quickly. What would he do if the manager dismissed him? No, that must not happen.

'Just to keep things in order,' he said. 'But I'm willing to see to everything. I have been at the bank for seventeen years, Herr Direktor. Never been absent for a single day. But to keep things in order, I thought, Herr Direktor. Everything might get muddled up.'

The manager of the bank was still looking at him.

'Well?' said the manager.

'If I could stay,' said Polzer, 'I mean . . .'

'As you like,' said the manager, turning away.

Polzer looked round the room uncertainly, then went back to his old desk.

'You're your own worst enemy,' said young Wodak.

Polzer was still very agitated. 'That's not impossible, Herr Wodak,' he said, 'that's not impossible.'

'It's all right for those who can do without it.'

Wodak sighed.

Polzer stood up. He went over to Wodak. 'Please, Herr Wodak,' he said, 'don't say that. Don't say that, Herr Wodak.'

When Polzer came home from the bank a few days later, Dora was sitting in his room with Frau Porges. Dora was crying.

Karl had been taken into hospital. Dora wanted to stay with him, but he had brusquely ordered her to leave.

'He's not a bad man,' said Dora, sobbing, 'no, no, I know him. And now they're going to cut his arm off as well. God, what will be left of him?! If you knew how handsome he used to be, Frau Porges. Who knows whether he'll survive it?'

'One must never give up hope,' said Franz Polzer.

'He's so weak,' said Dora. 'He only has to sit in his chair for half an hour and he's covered in sweat.'

'Sonntag says he's had worse cases to look after and they lived for many years,' said Frau Porges. 'Sonntag's a good nurse. Reliable. That's his great advantage, Frau Fanta. How much easier things would have been if Porges had had a nurse. What I went through in his last weeks, Frau Fanta! No, no, I wouldn't want that again!'

She dabbed at her eyes with her handkerchief.

'He's to be operated on tomorrow,' said Dora Fanta, crying. 'If only he comes through it! He's a good man, believe me.'

'We will not give up hope,' said Franz Polzer.

Polzer could not imagine how Karl would look without his left arm. That from now on just the right

arm would hang down slackly from the fat trunk was
something he could not conceive. At the same time
he could not get the amputated left arm out of his
mind. It seemed essential to find out what would be
done with it. Sonntag must know. He would be left
holding the arm after the doctor had severed it from
the trunk. Polzer was disturbed by the thought that
Sonntag might simply throw the arm away, just as
butchers throw the stinking entrails of slaughtered
cattle into a pit.

'What will Sonntag do with the arm after they've
removed it?' he asked.

Dora burst into a loud sob. 'Oh God, Herr Polzer!'
she said.

Polzer was disconcerted. Dora would not calm
down. He realised he had asked an inappropriate
question.

'What a thing to say, Polzer!' said Frau Porges.
'Don't cry, Frau Fanta. I'll make some tea. Tea will
calm you down, believe me.'

'No, no,' said Dora. 'I have to go. Franz will be
waiting at home. No, no, no tea. It's so horrible,' she
hid her face in her hands, 'it's so unbearable, oh God,
what will Sonntag do with the arm? Where will he
throw it, no, no! ...' She burst out into loud,
uncontrollable sobbing.

Frau Porges tried to get her to straighten up.

'Don't you trouble your head with that,' she said.
'Who cares? The arm's covered with ulcers, Frau
Fanta. What could Sonntag do with it? We'll ask
him tomorrow, Frau Fanta, what he did with the
arm.'

Dora stood up. She tidied her hair. She nodded silently to Polzer and Frau Porges and left.

The next evening Polzer rushed straight from the bank to the hospital. Frau Porges and Dora were in the vestibule. There was a smell of medicaments. Without a word, Polzer shook hands with the women.

Dora was not crying. Her eyes were dull, the lids reddened. Her features were pale and rigid. She stood there, unmoving.

Nurses, both male and female, went past silently in felt slippers. Frau Porges was reading the signs on all the doors.

Finally Sonntag came. He was wearing a white apron.

Dora did not go to meet him. She did not move.

'The patient is as well as can be expected,' he said.

Frau Porges asked whether she and Dora could go and see Herr Fanta.

'The doctor has forbidden visits for the first few days,' said Sonntag.

Dora opened her mouth. She spoke haltingly, as if the words were hurting, loudly and in a slurred voice. 'What has been done with the arm?'

The nurse looked at her. 'Limbs are buried in the yard,' he said.

Dora fainted. The nurse picked her up and carried her to an empty room. He laid her on a bed and unbuttoned her blouse. Frau Porges brought some water. The nurse moistened her brow. Then he pulled down the top of her slip and wet her left breast. He had short, fat fingers. Polzer left the room and closed the door softly behind him.

All the time he was in the hospital, Karl refused to have any visitors. Frau Porges, Dora, Kamilla and Polzer went every day. And every day Sonntag appeared, bowed and said he was sorry, but he could not take the ladies and gentleman in. The patient's condition was satisfactory but Herr Fanta did not want to see anyone. Dora said nothing. She stood there, half turned away, her eyes moving restlessly over the floor, her cheeks flushed. Polzer assumed she felt hurt and ashamed at Karl's refusal to see her. He wanted to tell her he was sure Karl was not yet accustomed to only having one arm and felt it was too horrible to let other people see him like that. He still found the image of the bloated trunk with the single, thin, paralysed arm hanging down all by itself beyond comprehension. Only now did the awareness of how much of a cripple Karl was really sink in, brought about by the idea of that single, withered extremity sticking out of the mass of fat.

On the way home he walked beside Dora. Dora was agitated.

'I have to talk to you, Herr Polzer,' she said. 'No, I'm not ashamed. I just can't stand it any longer, believe me. That man is so repulsive. His shaven head is so round! And have you seen his tiny nose and his small eyes? He's looking at me all the time, Polzer. I can't stand that vile look. He doesn't look me in the face, but here, at my breast. I'm afraid. I can't stand it any longer.

He behaves as if we were close acquaintances.

Since that time I fainted ... Oh God! It wasn't necessary, when I fainted, to undo my blouse and pull down ... Why did he do it? Why did you let him, Herr Polzer?'

Polzer said nothing.

'He's always looking at me, here. As if he could see through my dress. Please order him to stop. When I came to, Frau Porges was smiling. Sonntag pulled my slip back up over my breast. I can still feel his fingers on my skin. It was such a shock, I didn't dare move.'

She paused and looked at Polzer.

'Oh God, the things I'm telling you, Herr Polzer. But I have to tell someone. You must tell Karl the nurse has to go. Let him get another. He's always looking at my breast, I can't stand it any longer. Why did you let him, that time I fainted? Karl must understand. Tell him everything. I can't stand the idea that that person saw me and his fingers ... he didn't just do what was necessary, no, no, his fingers played with ... Tell Karl that, tell him everything.'

Polzer told Karl two days later.

The nurse came with the message that Karl wanted to talk to Polzer.

Karl's blanket had been pulled up to his chin. The blanket arched up from his neck over what was left of his body, then fell down, empty, onto the bed. Polzer looked away. He had never seen Karl in bed before. He shuddered at the sudden visibility of the chopped-off ends of this crippled body in the emptiness under the blanket.

Karl's face was pale.

But the eyes behind his glasses were bright.

'First of all get used to the sight,' he said.

The nurse in his white jacket and white apron made to leave.

'You can stay, Herr Sonntag,' said Karl, 'I can't have any secrets from you.'

'I don't know whether my presence is acceptable to Herr Polzer.'

The nurse spoke slowly and in a monotone. Polzer did not reply. The nurse bowed and left.

'You don't like my Sonntag, do you?' said Karl. 'And there'd be something funny about it if that dislike didn't go back to Dora. Is my angel stirring things up against him? Oh yes, I can well believe she's not happy with him. She's been shut out, you see, I don't need her any more. How long is it since I saw her? Goodness knows what's been going on in the meantime. I don't doubt she'll have started stirring things up against poor Sonntag as soon as possible. Because she loves me so much, of course. Because he's not the right man for me. She's already won you over, of course.'

'I wanted to talk to you about that,' said Polzer.

'About what?'

'About your nurse.'

'About my nurse? What about my nurse? Is this the first shot in the campaign?'

'Karl,' said Polzer, 'you must get rid of that nurse. Take a different one.'

'Why?' asked Karl. 'Don't you like his nose? His short, chubby physique? I tell you he's a splendid fellow. Reserved, only speaks when he's spoken to and then with a certain dignity. Hah, one would never believe he was once a butcher. I often get him to tell me about his work. He tells me how a calf is slaughtered and cut up, calmly, in a matter-of-fact way. What have you got against him? He's devout, goes to church a lot. That should incline you in his favour, Polzer. Or does Dora not care for him?'

'It's Dora who's asking you to get rid of him.'

'Aha, just as I thought, Polzer, just as I thought. She never imagined she could become so superfluous, so completely shut out. I don't need her any more. No, I don't, Polzer, especially not now. Was it she who put you up to this? Yes or no? She won't get anywhere with it, tell the sweet little thing that, Polzer, tell her that.'

'That's not it, Karl,' said Polzer.

'What is, then? What was the message she gave you? Come on, my lad, say your piece.'

Polzer stared at the floor. 'When you had your operation, on that day Dora fainted. Your nurse . . .'

'Well? Why don't you go on? Sonntag told me about it. He carried her into a room, lay her down, undid her blouse, pulled the top of her slip aside and moistened her skin with some water. I said to him, "So you've seen my wife's breast, Herr Sonntag. Well, what did you think of it?" And what do you think he replied? You'll never guess. "I know," he said, "it is not my place to comment on your lady wife's breast." Ha, ha, ha! What do you say now? Can I dismiss that man?'

'He did not just moisten it. With his fingers he played . . .'

136

'With her little breast? With those fingers, those stubby, red fingers. I tell you, Polzer, I like the man. Doesn't he look like a wild pig? A mixture of saint and wild pig? I'm sure darling Dora must be glad someone fancies her. What more does she want? Now she's got everything she needs at home.'

'He looks at her in a strange way. She says she can't stand the way he looks at her.'

'He likes her! Every man to his own taste. I like your Widow Porges. What does darling Dora want? Must it be a tenor and nothing else? Tell her she doesn't understand these things. Tell her she should have a closer look at Sonntag.

What kind of man is her tenor, anyway? I think he's afraid of catching a cold every time someone farts.

What a tender plant she is! She can't stand him, Sonntag, of all people, she who's had so much practice in putting up with things. No, no, tell her, Polzer, tell her Sonntag's staying. She can keep out of his way, if she doesn't like him. She doesn't have to come and see me, really she doesn't. I don't ask her to, never have asked her to.'

'But if she's living under the same roof with him, Karl?'

'That, Polzer, is what she will not be doing. That's why I wanted to talk to you. Or did you think I was just desperate to see you? I know you're a pastmaster at keeping people amused, but just at the moment I don't feel the need for urbane conversation. She won't be living under the same roof as him. When I leave here I'm not going home, I'm going to live with you. Discuss it with your Klara. And tell Dora I'll start screaming in the street if they try to take me to her apartment. People will take my side when they see my stumps. As soon as anyone asks why, I'll shout out loud that they're torturing me, they're trying to kill me. Remember that, Polzer, and tell her.'

'Can you do that to her?'

'Oh yes, I can do that to her!' Once again, he imitated Polzer's voice. 'And more! And more! Has she done nothing to me, little Saint Dora? Do I have to tell you again? The cut's healing nicely, tell her that, that'll cheer her up. She's terribly worried about me, I know. But I'm not going to die just yet. I lie here, stinking like a tub full of dung. But I'm not going to die just yet. There's all sorts of things I can do to her before the next arm goes, you tell her that. It'll be a while until then. She'll have to learn to be patient, will my dear wife.'

Frau Porges got the room with white dust-covers over the furniture ready for Karl and his nurse. When Polzer asked whether she had any objections to taking in Karl, she replied, 'In times like these, you have to make do with whatever turns up.'

During the nights Polzer tried to work out how he was going to tell Dora about Karl's decision. He met Dora every evening at the hospital. One day after another he put off telling her, knowing she would be devastated. He himself was afraid that Karl's moving in would bring great changes. Karl's presence, always talking, always wanting something, was bound to disrupt the established order in Frau Porges's flat. In addition to that, he wouldn't be alone. His nurse was coming too. The nurse was a stranger. No one knew him. Perhaps when Polzer was at the bank he would go through the rooms and use the opportunity to appropriate things. Polzer started to make a detailed inventory of all his things at night. To be safe, he noted everything he possessed down on a sheet of paper. His disquiet was increased by his uncertainty as to how Dora would take the move. He could not rule out the possibility that there would be violent arguments between Dora, Karl and Frau Porges. When she got worked up, Dora was capable of things which Polzer could only think of with horror. He had no idea what to do. Frau Porges did not seem to understand how serious the situation was.

When he asked her how she thought things might turn out, she said, with a shrug of the shoulders, 'We'll have to wait and see.'

Polzer wanted to explain that it would be too late for decisions if one waited until one saw. He did not do so because Frau Porges refused to respond to his hints. He sensed there were dangers lurking which he could not quite see and which it was too late to avert anyway.

Polzer suddenly sat up in bed. He thought he had heard horrible groans coming from the empty sitting-room. He hardly slept and even during the day he was filled with restless agitation. He would have liked to see the doctor, but the doctor seemed to be avoiding him. Polzer hoped a meeting with the doctor would calm him down. The doctor had brought agonies on him beside which his fears about Karl's move paled into insignificance. Perhaps the doctor could help him. Perhaps if Polzer gave everything back – the suit, the underwear, the hat, the ties, the shoes – everything would be all right again.

It was only with trepidation that Polzer entered his room at the bank in the mornings. If there was a smile on Wodak's face, he recoiled in horror, assuming he had been unmasked, his lie seen through. His pen faltered at every noise, at every footstep approaching along the corridor. Someone might come rushing in, confront him, tell him to his face that he was a liar, a beggar wearing clothes someone else had given him and pretending to be a rich man, drag him from his chair, mock and ridicule him. Herr Fogl would want to get his own back for the embarrassment he had caused him. Herr Fogl had made the speech that had been the talk of the department for days. Perhaps Herr Fogl would hit him. Franz Polzer knew he had to accept it because he was the guilty one. He would take his hat and run the gauntlet of laughing faces to the door. They would call out after him down the stairs and lean out of the windows to keep on shouting at him as he went down the street.

Franz Polzer looked at Wodak. Wodak smiled back at him. He considered leaping up and falling at the feet of the seventeen-year-old to beg him for mercy. He would tell him that he had not come into an inheritance, that he was poorer than everyone else in the bank; that he did not have a home, breathing space where he could find rest, that he suffered there as well, especially now when so much was brewing; that he was old enough to be his, Wodak's, father, and yet he had gone down on his knees before him, nor was it out of pride that he had said that, he had gone down on his knees willingly. If only people would forgive him! If only they would not torment him, if only they would stop terrorising him, they knew already, they knew he was a beggar, why did they go on toying with him like this? What was the moment they were waiting for? He could see the way they smiled, oh, him too, Wodak, his cruel son, he was smiling. Why was he waiting? If he demanded it, he, Wodak, then Polzer would leave and never come back to the bank, even though in these times it was so hard to make a living, he would go if he, the seventeen-year-old, demanded, so that Wodak would see his remorse, even though he knew himself that he was incapable of doing any work other than that which he had been doing for the last seventeen years, without missing a day. Always the same work in those seventeen years during which Wodak had grown up, gone to school, played, laughed, fought with other boys, chased girls in the park in the evening! He would do it, he would make that sacrifice, if only they would forgive him and put an end to his torment . . .

Franz Polzer heard laughter from the neighbouring room. He held his breath. His hand lay heavy on the paper . . .

Dora learnt of Karl's plan two days before he was discharged from the hospital. It was evening and she was sitting in Franz Polzer's room when the nurse arrived. He was carrying a heavy basket.

Dora looked at Frau Porges.

'Yes,' said Frau Porges, 'I've made up the third room for Herr Fanta.'

'Frau Porges,' said Polzer, 'you could still cancel it. Say the room's too small, say it's too much work for you –'

'You have to take what's on offer,' said Frau Porges sharply.

Dora stood up. The nurse was standing in the doorway. When he felt Polzer looking at him, he said, 'It is good to fulfil the wishes of the sick.'

He looked at Polzer as if he were answering a question he had asked. Franz Polzer felt revulsion at the nurse's oily voice and the way he spoke in a monotone. Dora had hurried to the door. The colour had drained from her face.

'I'll accompany you,' said Polzer.

Dora shook her head.

'It's only a short detour for me,' Polzer heard Sonntag's voice say, 'and it is inadvisable to leave a person by themselves in such a state.'

He followed Dora, who was already going down the stairs.

Next Sunday Karl was carried out of his hospital room. Waiting by the stairs were Polzer, Dora, Frau Porges and Franz Fanta. Karl was carried by two men. The nurse followed with a suitcase. Dora had not seen Karl since he had gone into hospital.

Karl, wrapped up in thick blankets, turned to her. 'You'll come and visit me sometimes, won't you, my little dove. And now you'll have the whole apartment to yourself, won't you.'

Dora sobbed.

'Just look at her,' said Karl, 'now she's starting to cry. And I'm doing it all for her sake. Believe me, Dora dear, just so as not to be in your way. You're young and beautiful, still beautiful in spite of everything. Oh yes, you are. You shouldn't have to restrain yourself, my darling.'

'Karl,' said Polzer, pointing at Franz. Dora was pressing Franz's head to her.

'Oh Polzer, what tact, what delicacy!'

What Polzer feared had begun. The door had been opened. Once order had been disrupted, ever increasing chaos was bound to follow. The breach had been made through which the unforeseen could pour in, spreading fear.

Now the cripple was in the room with the white-shrouded furniture. He could be heard groaning at night. The pus was eating deeper into his flesh and he was tormented by bad dreams. Polzer listened. Death was in the house, waiting. The nurse crept round the rooms in felt slippers. His footsteps could not be heard. It was a shock suddenly to find he was in the room behind you.

The nurse wore a white jacket and a white apron. The apron was tied round his waist underneath his jacket. It was not new. At the front it had a rust-coloured stain the size of a plate which drew Polzer's eye. Polzer knew the stain was a blood-stain, faded with age.

After only a few days a new change occurred. Now that the order had been disrupted, Franz Polzer saw no point in putting up resistance. There was no help for it, nothing to hold onto any more.

He was sitting with Karl one evening. Karl had been placed in a chair such as children who cannot yet walk have. This chair had been specially made for him. At the front it was closed off by a board so that Karl could not overbalance and fall out. In addition,

Karl's trunk was fastened to the arms with a strap. The stump of his left arm was bandaged. The bandage gave off a powerful smell. The solitary right arm stuck out of his trunk.

Sonntag had been sent away. Polzer was alone with Karl. Karl listened to hear if anyone was in the next room. There was no sound. Frau Porges was in the kitchen.

'Polzer,' said Karl. He spoke hastily and in a low voice. 'He can't stay in this room. You do whatever you like, but he must sleep in your room. He can't sleep here any more, Polzer. Let him sleep with you, or you move in with Frau Porges, but he can't stay here, Polzer, I'm afraid of him.'

Polzer was surprised. Hadn't Karl become attached to Sonntag?

'What's happened Karl? You were happy with Sonntag.'

Karl was agitated. 'He's in league with Dora. Haven't you noticed? If you only had eyes, Polzer! No, now she's overcome her maidenly modesty, she's not afraid of the way he looks at her any more. I've been aware of it for a few days now, Polzer, I'm not dreaming, they look each other in the eyes. I'm defenceless, but I can see the most surreptitious glance. I mustn't fall asleep. He's the man to do the job. Who'll be surprised if I'm found dead one morning? You, perhaps, you simple soul? A towel over my head and I couldn't even shout out. That would be the end of me.'

'You're doing her an injustice, Karl.'

'I have to be careful, Polzer, I have to be on the

alert. I'm defenceless. If I should fall asleep ...
They're in it together, Polzer, Dora and him, he's a
butcher, he's the man to do it. On her own she
wouldn't dare, no, no. She'd be afraid to do it. I'd
shout, she wouldn't have the strength, her muscles
would give way. But he's up to it, Polzer. She'll have
all that money and he'll get a nice pile. They're
already dividing it up in bed. Have you seen the red
stain on his apron? Do you know what it is, Polzer?'

Polzer said nothing.

'Blood, Polzer, old blood! I asked him. "It's an old
apron," he said, "that's calves' blood from when I
was still a butcher."'

Polzer recoiled.

'Calves' blood?' he said. He hadn't thought it
might be calves' blood.

'I don't want to be a calf, Polzer!' Karl screamed
with laughter and wobbled on his chair. 'Do whatever
you like. You can sleep with him. He won't do anything to you. Why should he bother with you? Take a
knife to bed with you and when he comes, stab him!'

'No, no,' Polzer begged.

'You're afraid? Then go in with Frau Porges. Sleep
with her. I want him out of my room today. My room
must be locked. Then if he turns the key in the lock
I'll wake up and can shout out. She shouldn't cele-
brate too soon. I'm cleverer than she is. Tell Frau
Porges you're moving your bed into her room.'

Franz Polzer nodded. He realised that everything
had started to slip out of control. Now he had to
live in the same room as the widow, always smell
her smell, always see her fat flesh, in the evenings,

when she got undressed, took off her corset and her petticoat slid down her body to the floor.

When the nurse came, Karl said, 'Herr Sonntag, it seems to me you ought to have a room of your own, a room where you can feel at home.' He smiled. 'I want you to feel happy here. Herr Polzer has agreed to give up his room for you. You can move in today.'

'Thank you for your kindness, Herr Fanta,' said Sonntag, bowing, 'and you too, Herr Polzer, for being ready to forgo your comfort for my sake. But I am not here for my own convenience. I am quite happy to stay in this room.'

'I can believe that,' said Karl. 'Your modesty does you credit, my dear Herr Sonntag. But it is my wish that you should have everything I can give you.'

The nurse made a silent bow.

When Polzer fixed the picture of St. Francis on the wall above his bed in Frau Porges's room, Frau Porges said, 'What's that picture doing here?'

Polzer gave her an astonished look.

'I don't want that picture in my room.'

'This picture?' Polzer asked in dismay. 'What have you against this picture.'

'It's ugly. I don't want any pictures of saints in here. No, it frightens me.'

'Frightens you? This picture? It's a plain, old picture, Frau Porges.'

'Take it down, Polzer,' she said. 'I don't want the picture. It's such an ugly picture. I feel frightened when I see it. I don't know what you people see in pictures like that.'

Polzer shook his head in bewilderment. What did

they all have against his picture? Why were the Jews afraid of it? Why did they hate it? Had the picture done something to them? Oh, perhaps it was wrong to live among people who hated and feared pictures of the saints? Karl hated them as well. Polzer could not hold anything against him. He had benefited from both his and his father's generosity.

Polzer did not respond to Frau Porges. Perhaps she would get used to it and not notice the picture in the morning.

The next day, when Polzer arrived back from the bank, he saw that the picture had gone.

'Where is the picture, Frau Porges?' he asked.

'Gone,' she said.

'The picture? No, surely not, Frau Porges.'

'Gone. I burnt it. I couldn't look at it a moment longer.'

'My picture? But I've always had it Frau Porges.'

His voice was trembling. He could not believe he didn't have the picture any more.

'And now you haven't got it any more,' she said. 'Go on, cry over it! if you loved me, you'd have got rid of it yourself.'

Franz Polzer said no more. The picture of St. Francis would not be over his bed during the night any more. Everything was going to collapse around him. He went to see Karl. He stood in the middle of the room. He did not see that the nurse was in the room. All he saw was Karl's horn-rimmed spectacles with the light reflected in the lenses. He felt he was about to fall.

'She has burnt my picture,' he said.

'Your picture? The picture of the saint?' Karl laughed. 'That really was careless of her. Now our St. Francis will be angry.'

'I've always had it. I had it when I was at school.'

'I know, I know. I can still see him. He was all the colours of the rainbow. Red, green, blue, gold. No house-painter could have done a better job! And now? You're devastated, yes? And I suppose you think he's going to avenge himself? Go on, admit it, that's what you think. I wouldn't be surprised if he did, believe me. And I wouldn't be surprised, either, to see you go out with a crown in your purse tomorrow, Polzer, and buy yourself another saint to protect you.'

Polzer shook his head.

Karl gave him a challenging look. 'You fool! You incorrigible fool! Off you go, d'you hear, off you go and buy yourself a replacement. A St. Francis the Second. Maybe you'll find one that's even shinier, Polzer. Then you'll be safe, nothing can happen to you.'

Polzer was amazed to see Karl become angry. He wanted to say that that wasn't it, to clear up the misunderstanding. But already everything seemed far away and insignificant. He could see the spot where the saint had hung in his mother's room. Above her bed on a wall with the whitewash flaking off. A rose had been stuck into the frame. Polzer felt very surprised. He could hear Karl speaking and sensed that the nurse with the red stain on his apron was slowly approaching. He had completely forgotten the rose and the whitewash flaking off the wall.

He shook his head in amazement, for the rose and the wall had been blanked out of his memory.

Karl said, 'If it were because you were God-fearing, now that I could understand, even though I'm not like that myself. But no, it's superstition, it's no different than that fuss with your penholder. Haha, Franz, do you remember that penholder?'

He laughed out loud, looking Polzer in the eye.

'That's not it,' said Polzer. 'It's just that I've always had that Saint Francis.'

He was afraid Karl would laugh again and looked at the floor. But the nurse had come over and was standing beside Karl's chair. 'A God-fearing person . . .' said the nurse in a deep monotone.

Karl gave the nurse a sharp look. The nurse broke off.

Karl gave him a smile of encouragement. 'Come on, say your piece, Herr Sonntag. I'm glad you want to join in our conversations.'

'With your permission, Herr Fanta, there's just one small thing I'd like to say. Forgive me if I can't express myself like an educated person. I left school early.'

Polzer saw the stain on his apron right in front of his eyes. It was the calves' blood. Polzer sat down and closed his eyes. The voice of the nurse in his ears was soporific.

'What I wanted to say,' the nurse continued, 'is that a God-fearing person respects the divine order. If God exists, then surely His order exists, even in the smallest parts, and surely we should be sad if this order is wilfully destroyed? And as for the picture of the saint, shouldn't we honour all those witnesses who fought and suffered for Christ, given that we regard pictures of our dead parents as sacred? Everything is founded on what came before, if you understand what I'm getting at, and so things happen to us and no one can escape what is laid down for him.'

'Yes,' said Polzer.

'We think everything is dark and inexplicable. But all at once the brightness dawns and we see that everything happens the way things are. There are no other ways than the ways to Christ. Everyone is following them but only the few know them. The saint in the picture bore witness to these ways. If we profess them, we bear witness for Christ.'

'Well, my dear Herr Sonntag, these ideas mean nothing to me. I'm not a God-fearing man. No, no, that's the last thing I need, to have to believe God is punishing me with pus and stench, and to beat my breast and hope for the life to come. Surely your good Lord can't require that, Herr Sonntag, not that!?'

'The day will come when you too will realise that you are following one of these ways. Even I didn't always know, nor you Herr Polzer.'

Polzer opened his eyes. 'It's just that he was always on the wall above my bed.'

'There! You see!' said Karl, laughing.

'One day we will all see it. God grant that you still have time to bear witness to it and that it is not in your last hour, Herr Fanta. For that must be hard to bear.'

'In that case I'll have to hurry, Herr Sonntag. It

won't be that long now. You have to admit though, Herr Sonntag, he's not using particularly pleasant means to lure me.'

'Life is not a punishment, Herr Fanta, it just seems that way to the ungodly. The only comfort is that we must do and bear the good along with the evil. The God-fearing man accepts it and delights in it, the ungodly rails against it. The time will come when we will all understand. Nothing happens that does not happen for Christ's sake.'

'No, no, Herr Sonntag. That's enough for me. To ask us to delight in it is asking too much, I think. But I'm pleased you yourself are so convinced and content.'

'I wasn't always, Herr Fanta. I wasn't when I was a butcher and slaughtered the beasts every day. I did my work, but there was something inside me, something, if I may put it this way, like a dark mountain. I did not go around with my comrades. I walked alone. I was violent and people were afraid of me. At that time I tried alcohol. Then I was injured during a brawl and spent a long time in hospital in a town in Moravia. In the ward was a picture of Christ. There were patients with me who moaned and groaned. I clenched my teeth. My wound ached and I did not groan. I cursed the sister, a devout young nun, who cleaned my wound and bandaged it. I used obscene words in her presence. But she kept coming to me, patiently, with a smile on her lips. Her submissiveness provoked me. I wanted to see her get angry and I thought out a plan by which I could offend her deeply. When she came the next morning I was going to throw the bedclothes back to reveal my lust and mockingly ask her to help me. But something terrible happened. She did not come that morning. She had been murdered in the most horrible manner. The murderer was never found. During that night a convict had escaped from the prison ward of the hospital. No one was in any doubt that he was the one who had done the deed. This led to my awakening. I had tormented her and even that morning, when she already lay murdered, I was thinking of tormenting her more. I looked for solace. She had given me books with stories from the lives and sufferings of the martyrs. Now I read them and realised that atonement is the only comfort and that atonement is not once and for all, but eternal. It is the constant renewal of atonement that is our comfort. I had found Christ.'

Klara Porges had come in. She was carrying a bowl with Karl Fanta's supper. The nurse took the bowl from her.

'When I came out of hospital, I realised I could not be a butcher any more. I tried with a calf, but when its warm blood spurted out on my hands and it looked at me with its uncomprehending, dying eye, I got up and ran off. I knew then that I had to devote my life to the sick, continue the work of the murdered nun from Prossnitz. My butcher's knife I placed on top of the things in my suitcase. Every evening I take it out to remind myself that I was a butcher and that atonement is never finished. I look at it and test the blade. And I am glad its sharpness remains unused.'

He had opened the lid of a black suitcase standing

in the corner of the room. He took out a big knife and balanced it in his hand.

'Look at it,' he said.

'Put it away,' said Frau Porges.

'Don't be afraid, Frau Porges. Put your faith in Christ and fear no weapon. Do not fear death. The light of reconciliation shines from the faces of the dying. Many have died in my arms.'

He leant down over Karl Fanta and held the spoon full of soup to his lips.

Karl sat up.

'And now?' Karl Fanta asked uneasily. 'And now? I'll be the next Herr Sonntag. What do you want?'

'Don't talk about such things,' said Klara Porges. 'I can't bear to hear people talk about such things. And take that knife off the table, Herr Sonntag.'

Dora came every day towards evening. She stayed alone with Karl Fanta in his room. Polzer sat in the kitchen with Klara Porges.

They often heard the sound of Dora crying in the room. Then she would come out with her eyes reddened and fixed on the ground.

Sometimes Karl Fanta shouted for the nurse, for Polzer or Frau Porges. But Dora held the door shut from inside and begged them not to come in.

'He wants to show her naked.' Klara Porges smiled.

'He torments Dora a lot,' said Polzer.

'What's the matter with her? He's like a child. Why does she feel embarrassed with him. I don't.'

'You, Frau Porges?'

'Yes, me,' she said.

At night they could hear Karl groaning. His room was locked from outside. The nurse's bed was in the room where Polzer used to be. The nurse stayed awake. He walked up and down with regular steps. He trod quietly. But Polzer could hear him. Frau Porges was restless too. Polzer saw her sitting up in bed, listening.

'Can you hear him at night?' Karl asked in a low voice.

Polzer nodded.

'He says he has visions that keep him from

sleeping. He claims he's wrestling with the Evil One. What does he want, Polzer, what does he want? He took the suitcase with the butcher's knife with him.'

Polzer did not get much sleep. The air in the room was saturated with a slightly pungent smell emanating from Frau Porges's bed. He often thought he was going to suffocate. The widow would not allow him to open the window. She was very worried about draughts.

She washed herself morning and evening. He saw the dark, naked gleam of the widow's heavy flesh. There were folds of fat over her hips. She would come over to him and laugh softly. 'Are you afraid?' she would whisper. 'Look at me, do you hear.' He could feel her warm breath inside his ear.

Her hands tortured him. She held his mouth shut to stop him crying out so the nurse would not hear, and pushed him into her bed. At night he saw the line of white scalp shimmering between the black hair on either side. She was asleep. He wanted to get up, to destroy the parting. He knew that then everything would be all right. He was afraid. But there would come a time when he stopped trembling and then it would happen. There would come a time when he would have to get up to do it and the very thought made him quiver. He would rise up and calmly go over to the bed where she lay with her loud, heavy breathing. Void of feeling, of thought, he would coolly bury his fingers in her hair and destroy the parting. Perhaps chop it off. Chop the parting off with Sonntag's sharp knife, perhaps.

In the mornings, before he left, Polzer went to see

Karl Fanta. Karl's chair had been pushed over to the open window.

Sonntag was tidying up the room. He took the chamber pot out, brought water for washing, fetched Karl's breakfast. Full of impatience, Karl followed him closely with his eyes. He waited until he had left the room.

'Well,' Karl asked in a whisper, 'what's happening? What's the matter with your tub of lard? I can hear her clattering about in the kitchen already, Polzer. What were you up to during the night with your widow?'

Polzer did not reply.

'Ah well, you're discreet, I'll say that for you, my lad. I can understand that. A man of the world! Haha, no giving away of bedroom secrets! A real gentleman leaves them where they belong, between the sheets.'

Sonntag came in. Karl remained silent until Sonntag had left the room again.

'Have you had her, Polzer?' He was very worked up. 'You must have her, do you hear? I want to have her too.'

'You?' asked Polzer.

'Yes, me! I've seen quite a bit already and I've not been disappointed. On the contrary, Polzer, on the contrary! Oh, she's clever, is your Klara, very clever, haha. She looks after herself and she looks after you. You too! Who would have thought it? But it's best that way. No misunderstandings. All goods have their price and the goods *are* good, aren't they, Polzer, eh? Not beautiful, you think? My little Dora's better, you think? Delicate, an elegant figure, is that what you think? Well I just hope our pious wild pig enjoys it. Do you know he's started holding prayer meetings, Polzer? What do you think of that? I have the feeling we're all heading for the wilderness – led by him, of course.'

Karl paused.

'No, no,' he went on, 'it's not the little rosebud breasts that do it, Polzer. It can't reside in beauty, Polzer, not there. It lies somewhere else. There are gourmets and there are gluttons, Polzer, you see what I'm getting at? You get fed up with beauty. All you can do is look at it. Please don't gawp at me like a calf. There are gluttons who want to eat a whole pig, not just vol-au-vents. Never mind gazing at flowers! It has to be a pig, Polzer! She's got an ugly belly, yes? Rolls of fat? You must see it when she washes herself. You tell me, if you can, what's beautiful about a flat, girl's stomach. Come on, don't you know? She's bloated, you say? Breasts, fat belly, flip, flop, flabby as a piece of tripe. But that's just it, Polzer, flip, flop, the mummy pig! You don't have to look at me like that, Polzer, I'm not a real man any more, I know that, but I like to have what fun I can, hahaha.'

His face was twisted in a grimace.

'Off you go,' he said, 'off you go, little boy, with your belief in beauty. Go and find yourself a girl like Dora used to be and get into bed with her, but make sure it has nice clean sheets! And don't stuff yourself with soft bread beforehand or you might spoil the magic with a stinking thunderclap!'

*

158

What is all this? Polzer wondered on his way to the
bank. She looks after herself and you too, Karl had
said. What was that supposed to mean? Did he make
the same demands on her with which he tormented
Dora, and did she want him to pay her for it? What
did she need money for? No, no, her needs were mod-
est and, anyway, her income had increased since Karl
had come to stay. She wouldn't be embarrassed, she
had said, and would do what he asked. Did she really
want money from him? What if Karl should get her
to move in with him, into his room, Polzer wondered.
But Klara Porges would not do that. That would
mean he, Polzer, would be all on his own again. In the
room next to the nurse, whose footsteps paralysed
him with fear at nights. And what was this suspicion
Karl had about the nurse's prayer meetings? Polzer
had already heard about them. At first the women
had gathered in Klara Porges's flat, but now they
met at Kamilla's. Dora went too. Sonntag wanted to
convert the women. He read to them and told them
legends from the lives of the saints. That was what
Polzer had been told. Dora was not keen to go, the
other women seemed to have persuaded her. Polzer
did not doubt she still found Sonntag repulsive and
that Karl's suspicions about her were groundless.
Perhaps Karl knew how baseless his suspicions were
and was only pretending in order to hurt her. For
some unknown reason he hated her.

For a brief moment it occurred to Polzer that perhaps Klara Porges might be uncovering her flesh to
the cripple while he was at the bank. The thought
was embarrassing. And what was the matter with

Dora, who avoided him? And Franz, whom he rarely saw now. Where was the doctor? Why did he not come? And what about the money Frau Porges was demanding from Karl? Where did the women's interest in religion come from?

There's no order any more, thought Polzer. I should have moved out while there was still time. He thought of the nurse's quiet footsteps in the next room during the night, the dried calf's blood and the knife. The picture of St Francis was no longer hanging on the wall. Now it was all too late.

Young Wodak was not at his desk when Franz Polzer came in. Polzer started work. Wodak's hat and thin walking stick were hanging on the clothes hooks. Where was he? Could something have happened? Might it be ... Polzer listened. Was that people talking in the next room? All he could hear was the monotonous noise of the machines. But now steps were coming along the corridor, voices. Polzer stood up. Now they were at the door. Polzer grasped the back of the chair behind him.

The door was flung open. Fogl and Wodak came rushing in, accompanied by other men and women. Fogl, his face bright red, came up close to Polzer. Polzer leant back. He knew. He knew everything. He wanted to close his eyes, but that wasn't permitted. For a moment he seemed to see Wodak's laughing face. Fogl was standing before him.

Now he had to keep his eyes fixed on his lips.

'There you are, in the suit from your inheritance,' said Fogl. 'And you let me make a speech? Do you know what you are? A fraud, that's what you are,' he cried. 'Gets a suit given to him – the tailor laughed fit to burst when he told Wodak – and gets me to make a speech, our Mr. Come-into-a-fortune! I take that as a personal insult. Do you know what people call someone like you? A confidence trickster! Yes! And you have the temerity to stay here . . . Herr . . .'

He came even closer. Polzer did not move. He stared at Fogl's lips. Now they would fall upon him, he knew, now Fogl would raise his hand and tear the suit from his body. The thing he feared had come to pass. Polzer's breathing was calm and regular. Now they would punish him.

But they did not punish him. Fogl slowly retreated. They looked at him as if they were waiting for something. Polzer realised he must leave, must quietly creep away. He let go of the chair and walked slowly, head bowed. He passed between them to the door. At the door he felt the desire to turn round for one last look at his desk. He also wanted to say that he had already checked the top sheet on his desk, even though he had not signed his initials. But already he was out in the dark corridor.

Frau Porges was astonished to see him.

'I won't be going to the bank any more,' he said.

She gave him a questioning look, but he found it difficult to talk about it.

'Something happened,' he said.

He tried to conceal it from Karl. He left the flat in the mornings as if he were still going to the bank. He did not dare go to the city centre, where he might meet people who knew him. He walked along the

bank of the river, towards the outlying districts. On
Sundays he now went to a small café where he was
not known. He would have liked to see the doctor and
ask him to take the suit back. But the doctor must be
away on his travels. Polzer gave a start every time a
passer-by noticed the brown, slightly cut-away
jacket and turned to look at him. He knew that his
fraud was not over. He had not stopped wearing the
jacket. He looked as if he were a man from the upper
middle classes, like Karl's father. He kept close to the
buildings. The man who saw through him might
always appear.

The fact that Polzer no longer went to the bank
didn't remain hidden from Karl for long.

'What's happened?' he asked. 'You're not going to
the bank any more?'

Polzer blushed and said nothing.

Karl laughed. 'I understand. You're rolling in
money, the pair of you, so why bother.'

'Karl,' said Polzer, 'what's all this about money?'

'"What's all this about money?" Listen to him,
the innocent little lamb! Get your Klara to tell you.
Perhaps she'll whisper it in your ear one night in
bed.'

The floodgates were open. There was nothing to hold
back the chaos any more. It was pouring down on
him from all sides.

Karl Fanta's gold watch, which had always been
on the table beside the patient, suddenly disappeared. Sonntag and Klara Porges searched for it in
every room in the apartment. They found it in a

black wooden suitcase where Polzer kept his underwear.

The nurse put it on the table. He looked at Franz Polzer.

'We found the watch in Herr Polzer's case,' he said.

Polzer only understood when he felt Karl's eyes on him. He stood up and tried to say something, but the nurse forestalled him.

'Herr Fanta,' said the nurse, 'in the name of Christ, I beg you to answer this one question. Can you recall having given Herr Polzer your watch to look after? Perhaps you forgot.'

'No,' said Karl, 'I never gave it to him. But what's the point of all this?'

'The point is, only that alone could have freed Herr Polzer from guilt. If you cannot recall having given it him, then there is no doubt he could not resist. Herr Polzer must have stolen the watch.'

'Such a valuable piece,' said Frau Porges.

'No! No!' said Franz Polzer, raising his hands in horror.

The nurse looked at him earnestly. 'It is not for us to judge,' he went on. 'We are all of us sinners and each of us has his own burden to carry. The lure of gold is great for a poor man, one, moreover, who has lost his meagre livelihood. We do not know what sufferings you have to bear, Herr Polzer.'

'No, no,' cried Polzer. He could not think of anything else to say. He took a step towards Karl.

'Now, now,' said Karl, 'don't get distraught. It's nothing to do with you. The evil spirit was stronger

163

than your patron saint. No guilt attaches to you. Get
your patron saint to do some gymnastic exercises
under Herr Sonntag's supervision, Polzer. Perhaps
it'll build up his strength. Herr Sonntag, the watch is
yours, after my death – assuming I die a natural
death, Herr Sonntag.'

Sonntag bowed.

'That's all right,' said Karl. 'I know money means
nothing to you. That is why I'm giving it to you,
Herr Sonntag. And you, Frau Porges, must forgive
Polzer. I'm sure he only did it for you.'

Frau Porges shook her head. She was weighing the
watch in her hand. 'A valuable piece,' she said.

'Now where's my supper,' said Karl. 'I'm hungry.'

Klara Porges and the nurse went out of the room.
Polzer watched them leave. He decided to turn round
and go to Karl to ask what all that had been about.
He did not understand. Karl shook his head to stop
Polzer from saying anything.'

'Close the door,' he whispered. 'Are they in the
kitchen? . . . You don't have to say anything. You
didn't take the watch. You haven't got the courage. I
don't know what's going on. But I'm afraid. There
are things happening. Someone could put their hand
over my mouth to stop me calling out, and I could do
nothing to prevent myself from being slaughtered
like a calf. People want money. From all sides people
want money. Anything for money. Tell me, Polzer,
what does your widow do with the money? Listen
Polzer, you mustn't go to sleep before he's in his
room. Before he's locked this room, d'you hear? He's
started staying here a long time in the evenings. He

stands there, head bowed, talking to me. And it's so monotonous, so soporific! Fear is the only thing that stops me falling asleep. I keep my eye on him in case he moves. He's trying to get at me with his faith. They're all in it together. Dora doesn't cry any more. She obeys without crying. She's found reserves of strength from somewhere. Sonntag says she's fortified by the faith. She wants money too. But I don't give her any. "Soon you'll have it all, Dora dear," I say. I think she won't want to wait too long. She'll want to get someone to speed things up a bit. Fortified by the faith.'

'I can't get rid of him,' he went on, after a pause. 'That would really set things moving.'

Polzer was sitting in his room. He was waiting until he heard the nurse lock Karl's room.

Frau Porges got into bed. 'It's a valuable piece,' she said. 'If one were to sell it . . . Porges had a gold watch too. But nothing like as heavy. Hardly half the weight. I got two hundred for it.'

Polzer listened to see if he could hear Sonntag's footsteps in the next room. All he could hear was Frau Porges talking, keeping her voice low. She wanted him to tell her he hadn't stolen the watch. She wanted him to stand up, look at her and say it out loud. But he was listening for sounds from the next room.

Frau Porges pushed herself up on her elbows. 'Polzer,' she said in a whisper, 'you can get some money.'

He looked at her. Her nightdress had slipped

down from her shoulders. There was an excited look in her eyes. Two inches above them the parting began.

'Tell Dora Fanta you know everything, Polzer. You don't have to say anything else. Tell her she has to give you money.'

Money, money, everywhere money. Money from Dora Fanta. Why money from Dora Fanta?

'For God's sake, Frau Porges,' he said, 'what's all this about money?'

'You think we don't need it? You always need money in times like these. In the old days . . . You earn enough, do you, Polzer? Tell her when she comes tomorrow. Wait on the stairs and tell her. Just say you know everything. She'll give it to you right away, Polzer.'

Polzer stood up. He wanted to ask what this was all about. He wanted Frau Porges to tell him. What Karl asked her to do and what she did to get him to give her money. He wanted to ask how the watch came to be in his suitcase. Karl was right, there were things going on. It was all connected. The door had been opened, order had dissolved into chaos. He ought to get away. Perhaps it was still possible. There must be another similar picture hanging in the kitchen behind the shop. He remembered it. He would have to go and get it, secretly, creep along the corridor while his aunt was asleep, and if the floorboards did creak and she opened her door, then he would have to fling himself at her, throw her to the ground and knock her out, stun her with a blow to the head, on her parting, get the picture despite everything. He had to know. Now. She was staring at him intently. She was waiting. What was she waiting for? Was she listening? It was completely quiet next door.

He opened his mouth, but before he could say the first word a shrill scream rang in his ears. Polzer's mouth stayed open. It was a scream before dying. Was that what she had been waiting for? What was it? Oh God, what was happening in the silence that had descended again?

Polzer jumped. There was a knock at the door.

'For the love of Christ, come with me.' It was Sonntag's voice.

Frau Porges leapt out of bed. She followed Polzer and Sonntag in her nightdress.

Karl was lying in bed. There was a faint smile on his lips.

'I was overcome with faintness,' he said. 'Now everything's all right again. Herr Sonntag was telling me about the wounds the martyrs suffered. He tells the stories so vividly, with such realistic gestures, you think you're being martyred yourself. A good story-teller. It made me overwrought. Forgive me. I'm tired. You can go now, thank you. Lock the door, Polzer. Good night.'

He nodded and smiled, but to Polzer his features seemed twisted in an expression of mortal terror. He felt as if Karl's eyes, in boundless fear, were begging him for help.

He went with Frau Porges into the room they shared. Everything was in chaos. She went towards her bed.

'The money, the money,' he said. His voice sounded hoarse. 'What is the money for?'

She was standing one step away from him. She looked at him for a moment. Then she let her nightdress slide to the floor. She was naked.

'Here! Here! This is what the money's for!' Frau Porges slapped her belly. She gave him a challenging look. He turned away.

'This is what the money's for!' she cried angrily. 'For this! Who'll look after it, eh? Don't you turn away! Here,' she grasped his hand, 'here, can't you see: I'm pregnant with your child.'

He gave her a blank, uncomprehending look.

She pointed to her bulging belly. 'Yes, go on, look at me! That's what the money's for: I'm pregnant.'

She got into bed and turned to the wall.

In the next room the nurse was walking up and down, treading quietly with regular steps.

'We'll have to think everything over,' said Polzer, stunned.

He listened. It was only towards morning that the steps ceased.

Polzer seized every opportunity to go out. There was nothing but unrest in the rooms of Frau Porges's apartment. The nurse would come in through the doors without a sound. Suddenly he was standing beside Polzer. He had not heard him coming. Karl would call and Polzer had to spend the whole morning sitting with him. The widow's confession had increased his bewilderment and confusion. The widow's cheeks were pale, fat and unmoving. But every day the terrible body, containing the fruit of his unwilling couplings, seemed to Polzer to have grown

After lunch he could slip out unnoticed. Karl was sleeping, the nurse was in his room reading accounts of the lives of the saints, Frau Porges was in the kitchen washing the dishes. Polzer went down to the river. He walked along the embankment upstream and would sit down if the sun was shining, always on the same bench. He wanted to set everything in order, put everything together again, for now there was no order, every moment brought something unexpected. It was impossible to be prepared. There was no regular routine for him to cling on to. Perhaps he ought to get up, even now, go to the bank, sit down at his desk and take up his work where it had been interrupted. There was no doubt that everything would be in chaos there, would be getting more chaotic all the time, just as at home.

The order of years in the files had been disrupted and was in disarray. There was some mysterious connection between the bank and home. He must go there and set things in order, then everything would straighten out at home as well. Someone was sitting at his desk now, determining Polzer's fate. It was he who was disrupting the order of Polzer's life. He left things undone, made mistakes, haphazardly piled disorder on disorder. Someone was sitting there, someone he did not know who was drowning him, Polzer, in confusion and disorder. He must get up, go to his place and straighten out the tangled threads.

The order has been disrupted, he thought. He sat on the bench and looked across the wide river. It has to be restored, to save everything. That is not being superstitious, as Karl maintains. God-fearing perhaps. For God is calm, certainty and order.

But at the same time Polzer knew he would not go to the bank. His presence would be an insult to Fogl and the others. They must not see him again. He could not prevent the man sitting at his desk from destroying the order his life had been grounded on so that everything collapsed. There was nothing for it but to let things happen.

At this point on the river the buildings were not close together. It was only rarely that someone walked past Polzer's bench. Behind him to the right was the big monastery, and to the left on both sides of the river factories, detached houses and fields were to be seen. Sometimes children came near the bench to play, adolescent girls and boys. If they showed no sign of moving on, Polzer would get up and slowly walk back the way he had come.

One afternoon when he took his walk, Polzer was astonished to see Franz Fanta sitting on his usual bench. Franz seemed to be waiting for him. He stood up when Polzer came into sight and went to meet him.

Polzer had not seen Franz for a long time.

Franz came to visit his father every afternoon, at the same time as Polzer went for his walk. Delighted to see Franz, Polzer shook his hand. He reproached himself for having neglected Franz for so long, for having forgotten him. He must surely have things weighing on his mind.

'I've come to talk to you,' said Franz. 'I knew you came here every day. I've been waiting for you.'

'What is it?' asked Polzer.

He looked at Franz. Franz was agitated. Polzer saw that he had changed very much during the weeks he had not seen him. He had grown. But his face had become pale and drawn and there were dark rings under his eyes.

'Are you ill?' Polzer asked, concerned.

Franz brushed his dark hair back from his forehead. 'No, that's not it,' he said. 'I'm not ill, yet. That will come, but we'll talk about that another time – or better still, not at all.'

'Why should it come?' Polzer asked. 'Because your father's ill? That's not to say you'll get ill. You have to be careful, Franz, that's all.'

'Forget it, Polzer. You're well in with Papa. Papa spends his time thinking about all sorts of things. He always behaves as if I were just a nuisance. Often he's quite rude. I think he would have every reason to be much, much more polite to me.'

'The poor man's in pain, Franz. You mustn't get angry with him. But . . . I could hint at it,' said Polzer.

Franz shook his head. 'No, no, that's not it.'

He looked at Polzer. 'I have to tell someone,' he began abruptly after a pause. He came closer to Polzer. 'Polzer, you're the only one I can tell. It's preying on my mind, Polzer. It's terrible, terrible.'

He put his head in his hands.

Polzer stroked Franz's hair. The agitation was beginning to affect him too. He felt that this boy beside him, whom he loved, was suffering.

'Tell me,' he said, his voice trembling, 'tell me.'

Franz straightened up. He kept his eyes fixed on the river.

'I've spoken to father's lawyer. He said father's perhaps not in full possession of his faculties. He's throwing his money away, he said. The lawyer's already discussed with some friends whether he should be certified or not. Does that surprise you, Polzer? Well, it doesn't surprise me. Do you know who's been withdrawing the money from his account? Go on, guess.'

A shock ran through Polzer. It was Frau Porges who had come to mind.

'You'll never guess, no, you'll never guess, Polzer.'

Franz paused.

'I have to tell you, Polzer. It's Mama who's taking his money out. She needs huge amounts. At first she

tried to get it from him. Now she uses a forged power
of attorney. Don't shake your head, Polzer. That's
what's happening.'

'I'm sure you're wrong about your mother, Franz.
Why should she . . . ?'

'Why? Read that,' he said.

He handed him a piece of paper. Polzer read: 'The
money must be here by the evening, or he will learn
everything.'

'I found the note in Mama's handbag. It was written by Frau Porges. I went to my mother and showed
her the note. Polzer, Polzer, it's awful. I can't tell you
what happened.'

He sobbed. Polzer took his hand. 'Don't cry,' he
said, 'don't cry, Franz.'

'Mama looked at the note, then at me. I don't
think she's really bad, Polzer, but . . . She drew me to
her and began to cry uncontrollably. You know, as if
she had something weighing heavily on her conscience. But I was seized with anger, or something
like that, and I said – I've no idea where it came
from, but I said, "You're having an affair with the
nurse." At that she leapt up like a woman possessed
and shouted that it wasn't true, who had told me
that, I shouldn't believe it, and she swore by all that
was holy that it wasn't true.'

He fell silent.

'How could you believe that!' said Polzer.

'She confessed,' Franz went on, speaking in a low
voice, 'that it was the tenor. You know him, don't
you, Polzer. It was Kamilla's fault, she said. Kamilla
invited her to tea. The tenor was there. Kamilla went

out, leaving the tenor alone with my mother. Polzer, Polzer . . . I can't get it out of my mind, Polzer.' He wiped the back of his hand across his brow. 'It was over, she said, but now she needed money,' he went on in a matter-of-fact tone, 'more and more money or Father would hear of it. She told me I couldn't help her, no one could help her, no, and she cried and begged me not to tell anyone.'

'Is this true?' Polzer asked.

Franz nodded.

Polzer could hardly believe it. Had Karl been right after all? How could their son bear it? 'Frau Porges . . .' he said.

'I told Frau Porges,' Franz interrupted. 'She got very excited. She ordered me not to say anything about it, or she'd tell Father everything. Father mustn't hear about it.'

'You poor boy,' said Polzer. He felt the need to do something to comfort him, to put his arms round him and draw him close.

Franz felt the warmth in Polzer's look.

He moved away from him slightly.

'You think I'm better than I am, Polzer,' he said, his eyes fixed on the ground.

This isn't the same Franz, thought Polzer. Franz, the sixteen-year-old schoolboy. Under the pressure of all these terrible happenings he's become a man.

'No, no, Polzer,' Franz went on, 'it's unbearable. What should I do? It disgusts me, everything. I feel like throwing her in the river, yes, her and me, Polzer. And now she's going to these prayer meetings. The nurse harangues them with pious words. It's driving her crazy. She's crying when she comes home. The women berate her there. The nurse told them to. He says she's a proud, rich lady. She needs to be brought down. The women feel sorry for her. But they obey. She has to pour the tea and is not allowed to sit down. They call her filthy names. Oh God, oh God, Polzer, it's more than I can bear.'

'Don't say that, Franz, God knows what sufferings she's going through.'

'Oh yes, what she's going through! Perhaps they spit and she has to lick it up off the floor, to demonstrate her humility. Why does she allow it to happen? Why doesn't she let all hell break loose? The nurse is a fool, Polzer, but an evil one. He always carries a small package wrapped up in brown paper when he goes to the meetings. It's kept on top of his suitcase. You should have a look and see what's in that package, Polzer.'

He stood up. 'Let's go,' he said. 'You can't help me, Polzer. No one can help me.'

They walked along in silence.

Why the money? wondered Polzer. Why money all the time? For his child, Polzer's child, was that what the money was for? She must tell him where the money was and he would give it back. He did not need that money for his child.

'She'll give the money back,' he said.

'Who?'

'Frau Porges.'

'Do you think she's the one that has it? And if she does give it back, does that mean Mama did not lie with the tenor on Kamilla's sofa?'

175

He stopped with a fit of coughing.

'Papa making his presence felt,' he said, breathing heavily. 'I won't be here much longer, Polzer. I'm going to get a doctor to send me to the south. I'm sick and tired of all this.'

Karl was already awake when Polzer returned. He heard Polzer come in and called for him. So Polzer could not go straight to Frau Porges, as he had intended. He was going to subject her to a merciless interrogation. He had not known that she took money from all sides, nor that the amounts she demanded were so large. Where was the money? Where did the money go? It wasn't to be seen anywhere, all that money, where did it go? Was she hiding it? Why did she need all that money for the child? He was going to press her until she told him everything, then take the money, go to Dora and give it back.

He went to Karl's room. The door to Sonntag's room was open. The nurse was not there.

'Where've you been all the time?' asked Karl. 'I want to talk to you, before Sonntag gets back. I sent him out, but he could be back any minute. I want you to stay with me in the evening until Sonntag goes to his room. I can't stay alone with him in the evening. I might fall asleep. Will you stay with me in the evening, Polzer?'

Polzer nodded. He looked through the open door into Sonntag's room. On the nurse's suitcase was the brown-paper parcel.

'They're all in it together,' said Karl. 'There's no

doubt that your widow's in league with them too, Polzer. By the way, Polzer, how ever did that happen? Who would have thought it, hahaha! who would have thought you had it in you! I have to give it to you, there's power in your loins. I couldn't believe my eyes! Though you're such an innocent, I wouldn't be surprised if you still didn't know she's pregnant. You're going to be a father, Polzer. Congratulations you lucky man.'

Polzer looked at the package. The nurse was not there. He could get up and go and see what was in it.

'And what next, Polzer, what next? I think your widow's getting all kinds of ideas. Will you lead her to the altar, Polzer? Till death do us part, Polzer? I think she's counting on you to marry her.'

'Propriety demands it,' said Polzer.

Karl laughed. 'Propriety demands it! Oh Polzer, Polzer, you're always good for a surprise! Propriety demands it! Where do you get them, Polzer? It's almost too good to be true. I could split my sides laughing if you weren't so exasperating! Propriety demands it and so Klara Porges will presumably become Klara Polzer. I just hope that won't affect relationships between us, eh? Between me and you and between me and her. You'll still let me have my little pleasures, won't you Polzer, even after you're married?'

'There's the package,' said Polzer.

'What package is that, Polzer? I can't see it. Bring it here, Polzer, bring the package here.'

Polzer stood up and brought it. 'The nurse takes it with him to his prayer meetings,' he said.

'Let's see what's in it, Polzer.'

Polzer's hands trembled as he pulled the paper apart.

At that moment the door opened quietly and the nurse came in. Polzer started. His hands dropped the half-opened package, which fell to the floor. A white, blood-stained butcher's apron rolled out. On the floor beside it lay Sonntag's butcher's knife.

Sonntag bent down and picked up the knife and the apron.

'Fresh blood,' said Karl Fanta in a toneless voice.

'That is the last blood,' said the nurse. As usual he spoke in a deep, calm monotone.

'What's the point of all this, oh God, what's the point of it?' asked Karl. His head had fallen back, his eyes were half closed.

'I wore this apron the last time I slaughtered a calf. I did not wash it, I kept it like this. Now I have everything prepared for our meetings,' said the nurse. 'The blood is on my breast and the knife sits on my thighs. That gives me the power to speak the name of Christ. For there is no other atonement than to take your sin upon yourself again, for it is never done with. When I wear the apron and carry the knife, I am once again the butcher I was, only aware now of my guilt. It is not given us to depart from our way and our sin. Thus attired, I renew my sin again and again in my mind. That is how, with Christ, repentance, meekness and shame in my heart, I atone for it through the humiliation of doing it again, despite everything, in spirit.'

He rolled the knife up in the apron.

'The sight of the blood and the knife makes all of us all more willing. I stand there, the knife in my hand, humbly willing to commit the sinful deed which is laid upon me. The women fix their eyes on it. They do not speak. I only speak a few words. They see the blood and the knife and come to know the pain of the martyrs. I test the sharpness of the steel. It is the knife of death.'

'What happens?' asked Karl. His face was pale. He was watching the nurse intently.

'We set up the crown of death and humiliate ourselves before one another.'

'Including Dora?'

'I do not deny her due respect, for she is your wife, Herr Fanta. She is a haughty woman, full of defiance and pride. Her body has been pampered by baths. But the symbols awaken her. She humbles herself by service. She stands and serves the meagre refreshments to those who are of poorer origin. Many more sufferings and humiliations await her, await them all, await me.'

He took his package and left the room.

Karl was breathing heavily. 'They're mad, Polzer,' he said in a low voice, 'they're all mad. That knife is behind everything. I believe he tortures them with that knife. Polzer, Polzer, could that blood be the blood of very special calves? But they would have to bear the scars! Frau Porges has no scars, Polzer. No, don't say anything, I know and I'm happy to to tell you I know, but don't say anything about it, leave it to me, Polzer, I know she has no scars. As for Dora, I don't know. The nurse is always in the room when she's here. But I mean to find out what calves that blood comes from. I mean to find out how far this applied humility goes, Polzer. I'll tell Dora I've had enough of my fatty diet and long for leaner fare, for her apple breasts. Then I'll find out everything, Polzer.'

'Don't torment her,' said Polzer.

'Don't torment her! Have you forgotten who brought all this on me? Who drove me out of my house? Who allied herself with all the others against me? Who keeps me surrounded? You can believe that innocent, childlike look if you like, Polzer! Just because they want money, they all want money. Why all that money?'

When the nurse brought Karl Fanta his supper, Polzer left.

'You are coming back, aren't you,' Karl called after him.

Polzer turned round and nodded. He felt Karl's fearful look.

Frau Porges put Polzer's supper on the scrubbed kitchen table. Since he had moved into her room he had to take his meals in the kitchen. The widow had tied her apron round her waist, making her condition even more visible. Polzer felt the moment had come to question her closely about the money. But he did not. She was sitting beside him, breathing noisily. He did not dare look up. If it were dark, he thought, if he couldn't see her, it would be easier.

He ate quickly and went back to Karl's room.

Karl smiled at him when he came in. The nurse had already cleared the plates away. Polzer sat in a chair beside Karl's invalid chair. The nurse stood in the middle of the room, his head bowed.

'I have told Herr Polzer what a gripping story-teller you are,' said Karl Fanta. 'Really incredible. I presume you don't object to him listening as well for once?'

'On the contrary, I'm glad Herr Polzer has come. I know that he is a secret ally, for he, too, is a God-fearing man.'

'Another superstitious one,' said Polzer, avoiding Karl's eye in his embarrassment.

'Superstition has its origin in the fear of God,' said the nurse. 'I feel that a person can only be superstitious if they believe in the divine order and cling onto small things, not daring to raise their eyes to God, serving him on the margins, if you understand what I mean.'

'A fear of God with obstructions in the way, so to speak!' Karl laughed. 'A shy fear of God, a bashful fear of God!'

'I can't express everything the way it is in my mind,' said the nurse. 'But perhaps I meant it the way you put it, Herr Fanta. I believe, if I may put it this way, that a God-fearing person can be superstitious and live out their fear of God through their superstition. I am surely not wrong in thinking this gentleman here will support me in my attempts to bring the blessing of faith to a sick man. He is a sinful man like myself. Just as I am a butcher and my path through life is lined with the lure of calves' throats, so along his path is the lure of the glitter of gold and he is possessed by the lust for money. Every one of us must bear their burden to the end.'

'Do you hear?' said Karl. 'You're possessed by the lust for money.'

'By the lust for money?' asked Polzer in a low voice. 'I haven't got any.'

The nurse looked at Polzer. 'We must bring our thoughts and our sinful deeds to life, again and again, for they are never done with, never expiated. Only in that way can we bear them to the end. I tell of my sins so that I may suffer them anew and bear them to the end. I tell how the calf is grasped, where the knife is placed, how the blood spurts out, how the skin is stripped from its legs. I gird myself with my knife . . .'

He made a move as if to go and fetch the knife.

Karl Fanta looked at him intently. 'No need to bother with that,' he said quickly, 'no need to bother with that.'

'I often show it to the women. In that way I suffer it once more.'

He was silent for a moment and looked Karl and Polzer straight in the eye.

'I feel that I am standing here before you in order to humble myself and to confess the thing I cannot confess to the women. To do so would be to offend against chastity. I beg you, mock me and curse me once I have confessed it. I want you to see how great and yet how puny my humility and my desire for atonement are.'

He took a deep breath.

'When I was young, seventeen, a man offered me money to go with him. The man was well-dressed and I did not think there was any danger. I was lured by the money, so I went with him. We went to an apartment where there were several men. They were all well-dressed, you could have called them gentlemen. They gave me wine to drink. Once I had drunk a certain amount they asked me to take my clothes off. I refused. They pressed me to do it, but I stood by my refusal. Then they left me alone. I was sitting in a corner. There was some wine in front of me. The men were drinking to each other and ignoring me. Then the Lord abandoned me. I had continued to drink. I stood up. I went into the middle of the room. They all watched me as I removed my trousers and stood before them like this.'

The nurse had opened his flies, exposing his penis. With a frozen expression on his face, he stared at Karl Fanta. Polzer did not move. He closed his eyes.

The nurse was standing in the middle of the room, his head bowed. He had not raised nor lowered his voice. More quietly, but in the same monotone, he went on, 'I confess it and do it again. I stand before you in dreadful shame and humiliation. Thus I suffer my sin once again. I expect you to curse me, to deride me and mock me.'

The nurse fell silent. He stood there, head bowed, appearing to wait. Karl waved his hand. 'Put it away, Herr Sonntag,' he said, with an uncertain smile.

The nurse did up his flies.

'If one had to commit every sin twice,' said Karl slowly, 'then a murderer would have to murder twice just in order to confess and humble himself?'

'I don't know,' said Sonntag. 'Though there might be some examples of that,' he went on after a pause.

'People say the Jews murder Christian children and
virgins. I do not hate the Jews. They say they do it
around Easter, at about the same time as they murdered Christ. It seems to me they have to do it again
and again, in order to suffer that deed again and
again.'

'What's all this nonsense?' said Karl. 'Do you
believe those fairy tales? No one can prove it, it's
never been proved. How do you know?' He spoke
angrily.

'It is known for a fact,' said the nurse.

'Known for a fact? How can you say that! Who
knows it for a fact? Who's seen it? Do you know it for
a fact, Polzer?'

'When I was a child people used to say that,' said
Polzer.

'Did they? So someone told you about it, did they?
And you believe it of course, do you, Polzer? Well
isn't that the limit! You think I, for example, or
other people kill children at Easter, do you? Why do
you live with me then? Come on, tell me?'

Why do I live with him, wondered Polzer.

'No, no,' said Polzer. 'you and your father have
been good to me, I know. It's a prejudice in the
countryside.'

'A prejudice in the countryside.' Karl imitated
Polzer's voice. 'Thank you for that, Polzer. Exactly.
It's a prejudice in the countryside. I can't argue with
that.' He gave Polzer an angry look.

'I didn't mean to offend you,' said the nurse. 'All
I wanted to say was that everyone is driven to
return to their deeds, again and again. People say

some dark force compels murderers to talk about their crime, even when it might lead them into great danger. God compels them. If I had murdered someone with my knife, for money, a woman, I assume that would be the case and I would be driven to tell how, while she was sleeping, I held her nose tight with my left hand for a moment. Then her chin lifts up for a moment and the skin stretches over her throat. The skin has to be stretched if it's to be done with one stroke. It's fat and folds can easily form. Then you cut across it quickly with the right hand. It has to be done at once, for scarcely has the chin been lifted than it drops down again. The knife has to be placed firmly on the skin, so it doesn't just slide over it. You can cut the head from the body with one stroke.'

'Oh God!' said Karl. 'What a thing to say! You put the fear of death into us, Herr Sonntag.'

'You're afraid? You don't need to be afraid, Herr Fanta. The Saviour is close by. I know you will not go to Him without faith.'

'Still plenty of time for that, Herr Sonntag.'

'Do you think so? Death can come to any of us, at any moment. How soon then might he come to you who are ill, Herr Fanta? He has already tapped you on the shoulder. Confess Him who suffered for you, before it's too late, so that you too might be saved. Herr Fanta, death is at the door.'

He took a step towards the door. Karl's face was frozen in a grimace of horror

Polzer stood up. 'What are you doing?' he said. Horrified, he put his hand on Sonntag's arm.

The nurse turned to face Polzer.

Polzer did not let go. The nurse's piggy eyes looked at him. 'You have not reached the end yet either, Herr Polzer,' he said. 'Perhaps the day will come when you, like me, will stand before the two of us and confess.'

'I don't know . . .' Polzer said falteringly.

'You don't know what you should confess? You know nothing of your lust for money? Think of the watch we found in your suitcase. And why do you want to find out from Frau Porges where she keeps her money? Maybe it really is only your curiosity that's driving you. It lures you and it draws you on. But then, when you know where the money is, evil will have you in its grip and you will seek to get your hands on the money.'

'No, no,' said Polzer.

Karl had closed his eyes. The nurse went over and undressed him. Then he wrapped his arms round Karl's trunk, lifted him up and lay him down on the bed.

'I'm tired,' said Karl.

They left, locking the door from the outside.

In the dark hallway Polzer sensed someone standing beside him.

It was the nurse.

'She hides the money,' he whispered, close to Polzer's ear. 'Perhaps she buries it. She gets money from all sides, from Frau Fanta, from the master, from Franz.'

'From Franz?' asked Polzer.

'Perhaps from other people. Tomorrow afternoon

just go as far as the monastery, then come home. I'll open the door for you quietly, Herr Polzer.'

Polzer went to his room. It was dark and Frau Porges was asleep.

Polzer turned back at the monastery. He set off for home. The whole time since the previous evening he had been restlessly going over in his mind what the nurse would have in store for him if he returned early from his walk.

At Charles Square he started to hurry. As Polzer reached the top of the stairs the door to the apartment opened noiselessly.

The nurse grasped his arm and quickly drew him inside. He put his finger to his lips. Polzer gave him a questioning look.

'He has to give her money.' Sonntag whispered it so softly Polzer had difficulty understanding. 'All of them have to give her some, the tenor, the student, God knows who else. Come.'

They were outside the door to Polzer's and Frau Porges's bedroom. The door was locked.

The nurse raised his foot and gave the door a violent kick. The lock burst with a crack and the double doors parted before Polzer.

Polzer heard a cry. He recognised the widow's voice. She was standing in the room, naked. She bent down, picked up her slip from the floor and held it in front of her.

Polzer did not move. He did not look at Frau Porges. The widow gathered up her clothes and ran past Polzer into the kitchen.

Polzer looked at Franz Fanta. He wanted to turn

round and see whether the nurse was still behind him, but he could not take his eyes off Franz Fanta. Franz Fanta was standing back against the wall between the windows. His head was leant back slightly, his eyes half closed, as if he were waiting.

What is going to happen, wondered Franz Polzer. What are we waiting for?

It seemed to him that he had already seen Franz like this. Once, many years ago, had they not kissed and embraced each other amid tears? And had he, Polzer, not been waiting, waiting all these years for the other to kiss and embrace him again? Yes, that was what he had been waiting for. It was all like a long-lost dream. Where were those limbs, in the yard of which hospital were they buried? He had dreamed of an ugly name, of a repulsive name, of the bloody wounds of his pregnant wife. The whole night through he had pressed his trousers under books and polished his shoes in the morning. He only had to keep his hands hidden. Oh, now the naked boy was lifting up his hands before him, as if he were afraid. Oh, he was still susceptible to shame, to feeling!

His coat was hanging on the wall. Hesitantly, Polzer stepped into the room. Franz Fanta had hidden his head in his hands. His back twitched. He was sobbing.

'Don't be ashamed,' said Franz Polzer.

He wrapped the coat round him.

He saw Frau Porges standing in the kitchen, already dressed. Slowly he went to join her in the kitchen.

'Come!' he said. He felt nothing inside.

She looked at him, questioning.

'Come!' he repeated. 'You don't need your hat.'

They went out into the street. She wasn't wearing a hat. He saw her without a hat and was surprised that it did not remind him of anything. There was no fear in him, no hatred as he looked at her. Nothing stirred inside him.

It's good she's not wearing a hat, he thought. We're ordinary people, he thought. We have to wear poor clothes, have to! That's the cause of all this. Better for us to tear up our good clothes than to wear them, he thought.

They went to a small café. They sat down at a table over by the wall. She sat opposite him. Her face was fat and pale, like the face of a corpse. Her eyes avoided his gaze. He looked at her calmly. The wind had tousled her hair at the temples. Where had this all happened before?

He knew he would start to speak now. 'What was that?' he said. He heard the sound of his voice as if it belonged to someone else. It was as if he had never heard his own voice before.

She dabbed her eyes with her handkerchief.

'Don't cry,' he said.

She shrugged her shoulders.

'I want to know everything,' he said.

He looked at her in silence.

'Stop torturing me! Don't look at me! Don't look at me like that! You know already. Why do you have to ask?' she said.

She pressed her face into her handkerchief.

'I want to know how it happened,' he said.

She shifted in her chair. 'How it happened . . . What's the point . . . He kept looking at me . . .'

'He's still a boy,' said Polzer softly. 'I loved him very much.'

He did not move a muscle.

'How it happened,' he said.

'God, stop torturing me! What do you mean, how it happened? How do these things happen . . .'

'Everything,' he said.

He leant forward over the table. He looked at her face. He was horrified by the face. How did this face come to be opposite him? This pale face!'

'I've told you everything.'

Why couldn't he get up and leave? What tied him to her?

'Everything . . . You must give me everything . . . The money . . . Why do you want money from him? . . . And the others . . .' He raised his hands. She saw his contorted face. 'They've all had you, all of them, the student, the tenor, the men from the bank, even Karl perhaps. And who else, who else?'

'It's a lie!' she exclaimed. She avoided his eye. 'Whoever told you that's lying! Whoever told you that is lying and I hope the lie sticks in his throat!'

'Swear that he's lying.'

'I swear. Now leave me alone.'

'I'm not going to leave you alone,' he said. What is it to do with me? he thought. 'No, no, I'm not going to leave you alone. Swear by your mother. Swear by your mother's dead body,' he said. 'Swear: may her ashes be cursed if he told the truth . . . You're not saying anything? Why aren't you saying anything? Why won't you swear?'

'Stop torturing me,' she said, sobbing.

'So you refuse to swear to it? So it was the truth I was told.'

She said nothing.

'Admit it,' he said

'But you know already,' she said in a low voice.

Then Polzer realised she belonged to him.

He dropped his arms. What should he do? What could he do now?

'All of them,' he said, 'all . . . oh God!'

She was in tears.

He saw the dark down on her lifeless fat cheeks. Like a corpse, he thought. He knew that she was ugly. Now he could never get away from her. She had black hairs between her breasts.

'Who else?' he asked quietly.

'No one, no one. Oh God, do stop torturing me.'

'Swear it,' he said.

'I swear.'

'No, not like that. "May the child inside me be born a misshapen cripple, may it be eaten away by leprosy in the womb." Swear that oath!'

'No!' she said. 'No! No!'

'Not all of them.' He slowly shook his head.

'To suffer such injustice . . .' She sobbed.

'And the child,' he said. 'And the child.'

Soon the child would be there. Soon this belly would open wide. Who had made this belly swell up like that? She must tell him everything, he would tear everything out of her, he must know everything,

for now she belonged to him, now he could never get
away from her, she was part of him like his red
hands, until her dying day, until his dying day, day
and night, he had to torture the shame out of her, all
of it, and bear it, again and again. She should never
wear a hat again, always go bare-headed, like a
woman serving in a shop, that was how it had to be.
He had been thrown out of the bank. Why, he wondered, why did they throw me out of the bank? Now
all this has come down on me.

He looked at her in silence. She dried her tears.

'I've told you everything,' she said. 'That's
enough, Polzer. Everything's over and done with. It's
your child, Polzer. We'll get married. Everything will
turn out all right.'

He stood up. 'Yes, yes,' he said.

That night Polzer did not sleep. He sat up in bed. He
heard the nurse's footsteps in the next room. He held
his breath and listened. Who wanted something from
him? What did the nurse want from him?

Sometimes he heard a deep sigh. Like a dying man
sighing. Was it the nurse who had sighed? Polzer felt
like screaming, but all that came from his throat was
dry breath.

He did not close his eyes. In his ears he could hear
the monotonous voice of the nurse. Where had he
heard it? 'Evil is not there for the evil man. Nothing
is there for him. Even evil is there for the God-
fearing. Only the God-fearing man can bear it, that is
what grace is. So he does not avoid it, but takes it
upon himself when it is there. For he has to keep

committing his deed and suffering until it is done with.'

The footsteps stopped.

Frau Porges was asleep. She was lying on her back. She couldn't sleep on her side any more. Polzer could not see her in the darkness. But he knew the arch of the blanket over her body up to her neck. And the parting above it.

He sat in bed, staring fixedly at the spot where her breathing came from, trying to pierce the darkness. During that night everything went through his mind, everything was alive, simultaneously and in sequence. Later it had gone. Sometimes a moment from that night would light up for him, like a forgotten word spoken again. He felt as if it were a stone beneath which something terrible was buried. As if in a dream, he struggled agonisingly to roll the stone aside, but it was as if it were giving way in every direction and yet not moving.

It was silent. Only her breathing. But wasn't that something creeping? Along the hall and into the room? Oh, nothing was fixed any more, everything had come apart, there was no order, no permanence!

What was that creaking? Had the wardrobe creaked? Was it not a footstep on the floorboard making it suddenly creak? A creeping footstep, a murderer's footstep? Other doors could be heard in the building, doors opening and closing. What was creeping through the darkness? Should he get out of bed, stand quivering by the doors, listen and feel in dark corners with his hands?

Was there a murderer in the house?

His eyes were smarting. He did not move. Klara Porges was sleeping. Why was she sleeping? Could she not hear it? What was it she had said? 'Everything's over and done with. Everything will turn out all right.'

Nothing will be all right, nothing is over and done with. Everything is still there and everything is awake, how can it be over and done with! The picture of the saint is no longer hanging on the wall by the bed as at home. That is over and done with, but the night is not, not the night when he was lying in bed and heard the creak of footsteps and he was in the hall and the door opened and the naked shadow was there and his father. Nothing is over and done with. But she, the pregnant woman, was breathing as if it were, as if that thought no longer existed, that terrible, unthinkable thought that was suddenly there. Her belly was breathing with her. The child in her belly was breathing, the living child. Soon the belly will be opened and the child will be lying in front of Polzer, naked, with limbs like tubes and deep folds at the joints, a girl with a line between her thighs. No, no, that wasn't what he wanted. He didn't want all that, it ought not to be. But all that had to be because nothing could be over and done with. She was ugly and everything was a torment. But everything had to be a torment and everything had to be ugly. Yes, yes . . . It would only be his if it was ugly, he was ugly himself, with red hands – oh God, why had he accepted the new suit? – he had sold pickled gherkins to the serving girls and his aunt had grasped him with the nails on her fingers while his father beat him, and Milka had grabbed him on the staircase. The blanket arched over her belly and the parting was above it. Whose was the child in her belly? All of them had abused her. That meant she belonged to him. But it was not over and done with.

He was going to get up, wake the pregnant woman. He was going to put his face right in front of her head, her parting, and, and . . . 'Nothing is over and done with,' he would say. It wasn't done with. 'Tell me!' She must tell him everything. How she had seduced the boy, had lured him on . . . the boy knew nothing . . . how she had grasped him, pulled him to her. And the others, she must tell him everything about all the others, she must squirm and tell him how they had lain on her, where they had touched her with their hands, here, there, this one, that one, exactly what each one had done, how they had done it, how often and how long and how she had panted and groaned, she must tell him everything.

He would pull the blanket back and see her. The swollen belly, the hairs between those breasts that slumped to either side when she lay down, the fat face, the hands that had felt all the men, all over. She was ugly and abused. Her body was yellow. But that was the way it had to be. She had lain underneath them, under all of them. And all of them had used her, but each one in his way, in his own way, and she must tell him about each and every one of them: like this and like that. And by whom this body was great with child, and whose child it was. He ought to uncover her and see her body. Oh,

everything was ugly and a torment, but it could not
be otherwise.

The student, the tenor and all of them, one after
the other, no, it must not be over and done with, it
had to be borne to the end. She was still sleeping. But
now he got up. He stood beside her bed. The blanket
arched up to her neck – where else, oh God, where
else had a blanket curved up in such a terrible way
over a belly? – and there was the parting. He would
pull the blanket away to see the belly in which the
child was lying, the child with the monstrous, open
slit-line between its thighs, the child in the abused
belly, on top of which they had all lain, every single
one of them on top of his child, on its belly. A belly
that ought to be naked, as it was when she held it out
to Karl, to his hand, for him to feel it.

He listened. No clock ticking. Nothing moving.
The night was passing. No doors opening softly.
Everything was sleeping. The footsteps were sleeping, the alien building was sleeping, the knife was
sleeping, the apron with the calves' blood was sleeping. Klara Porges was sleeping. Her head was on the
pillow, turned to the wall. The parting was there,
white between the black hair on either side. Nothing
was over and done with. That was not over and done
with either, the parting had been there always, the
parting with which the wind would wreak havoc, for
she was not wearing a hat.

She beat him and she tormented him and she had
always beaten him and locked the bread away. But
now he could destroy her parting. She was sleeping.
He could take this pin out of the knot, this one and

this one, and it would fall apart. He must do it quietly so that she did not wake up.

The knot came undone. She did not move. She was breathing deeply. He took hold of her hair. He wanted to cover up the parting. A rustling noise came from under the hair. He let go of it. It spread out. There was money lying on the pillow.

Polzer did not move. He looked at the money. That's the money, he thought. That's the money. Of all places, the money was behind her parting. Money for her belly. Her ears were uncovered. He had never seen her ears before. The edges were not curled but flattened out. They were flattened ears. They were yellow as church candlewax, dead, flattened ears. Her nose could be held closed for a moment with the left hand. Then the skin would stretch over her throat. The throat had to be stretched, because the skin was fat and folds could easily form. He gave a start. It had lasted too long. She shook her head. She had opened her eyes. She had said something. It sounded like something spoken in sleep.

He waited. His head was bent down over her. Now she had gone back to sleep. Her breathing was deep and regular.

In the morning Polzer slipped out of the room. He closed the door quietly behind him.

He went into the nurse's room. The nurse was getting washed.

Karl was also awake.

Polzer went over to his bed. 'She keeps it in her

hair,' he said. His voice was hoarse. He dropped onto the chair.

Karl and Sonntag looked at him. He was pale and his feet were trembling.

'The money,' he said, 'the money.'

He stood up. 'I have to go,' he said.

He felt his way, as if he could not see, until he found the door.

Two hours later he was standing outside the building. The concierge's wife was sweeping the entrance. 'What's that bag, Herr Polzer?' she asked.

'I found it on the stairs,' he replied. 'someone lost it.'

'That's Frau Porges's headscarf,' she said.

'Then she wrapped something up in it and lost it on the way home. A cabbage perhaps.'

'It's covered in blood,' she said.

'A calf's head perhaps, then,' said Franz Polzer, 'or something like that.'

He went up the stairs and into Karl's room.

'Well then,' said Karl, 'what's all this? You must have had bad dreams last night, Polzer.'

'She keeps the money in her hair. That's where she keeps the money. Where's Herr Sonntag?'

'He's gone out. He always goes to church in the mornings. He should be back soon.' Karl leant forward. He looked at Karl's lap where he had the bundle. His eyes flickered.

'Stupid as a calf, that's what you are, Polzer,' he said, 'stupid as a calf. I can't save you. You know how to kill a person, he explained it to you clearly. You hold their nose shut. You'll come to it in the end too. I know more, Polzer, but I'm next, look at me, Polzer, look at me.'

'What's the matter?' asked Polzer.

'Shh,' said Karl. 'It's every man for himself. We're all in for it.'

He closed his eyes.

When Sonntag came, Polzer was still sitting beside Karl.

'What's that you're holding?' asked the nurse.

'Oh yes,' said Polzer. He was still holding it on his knees. 'She wrapped something up in it and then lost it. I found it on the stairs.'

'May I see what it is?' asked the nurse.

He pulled at the bow in which the ends of the cloth were tied. He lifted up the scarf and Klara Porges's head rolled out of Polzer's lap onto the floor.

The knot her hair had been tied in was undone. But the parting was still there. Polzer saw it clearly, for the head was motionless on the floor in front of him, standing on the stump of its neck.

Karl gave a cry. It rang in Polzer's ears as if it came from a long way off. But he could not tear his eyes away from the head. Then the nurse wheeled Karl into Frau Porges's bedroom. The body lay across the bed, headless and half naked. When Sonntag returned with Karl, Polzer heard them talking.

'How horrible,' said Karl. 'How horribly ugly.'

'Beauty, Herr Fanta,' was the nurse's response, 'cannot be seen any more once people are dead.'

Polzer wanted to stand up but was unable to. How

long was this going to go on? He looked at the head. The lids were half closed. It was as if the eyes were squinting out of narrow white slits. Someone should take the head away, right away, so that everything would be over.

Karl sat up. He was breathing audibly. He looked at the nurse. The nurse was standing, head bowed, in the middle of the room.

'Help!' shouted Karl. 'Help! Something must be done. The head . . .'

'We must leave everything as it is until the police come,' said Sonntag, the nurse. 'That is the rule. Your wife will be here soon, Herr Fanta, then I'll go and make the necessary arrangements.'

The nurse had gone to Frau Porges's room. Polzer felt Karl's eyes on him. Yes, yes, something had happened. If only he could remember what, but it must have been too long ago. Now everything was forgotten. The nurse came back. You could not hear his footsteps. Just at night the floorboards creaked under those footsteps. He was holding the knife in his hand. There was blood on the knife. Why did they not clean it? Karl gave a sigh and let his head sink back.

'This is the knife,' said the nurse. 'This is what you did it with, Herr Polzer.'

'Put it away,' said Karl. 'What are you doing with the knife?'

'Where is the money?' asked the nurse.

Always the money. Now it was clear. Someone had cut her head off at the neck. Who? What had the nurse said? Was it true? Was it he, Polzer, who had done it after all? The hair in which the money had been was undone, but the parting was not destroyed.

The nurse raised the knife and spread his arms wide.

'Christ,' he said, 'Christ. We commit our sin for His sake. Evil exists so we will be brought low, so we will suffer our sin again and again. This sin is your sin, and there is no deliverance from it in this world.'

He put the knife in Polzer's hand. 'Continue to atone for your deed.'

Polzer stood up. Why did they not cover up the head and stop it squinting at him. Polzer looked at Karl. Karl's mouth was open. His face was rigid. He ought to pray, thought Polzer. What did the nurse want from him? Oh God, there was something dark, like a stone, inside his head. Something terrible had happened. He ought to remember. Earlier on, when he was sitting beside Karl, before the nurse came in, Karl had said something. He could hear the sound of Karl's voice, but he could not remember. Just that she had yellow ears, yellow as wax, ears like a corpse, that he could remember. He had seen them. But now all that was over and done with. Perhaps he would go back to the bank, every morning. Now she was gone. There had been something about a child, a female child. Now she had been killed. Hold the nose shut with the left hand, then the skin stretches over the throat. It had to be done quickly, because folds could easily form. Oh God, perhaps it could have happened like that.

Polzer was standing in front of Karl. He had the knife in his hand. Behind him the nurse had sunk to the floor. The beads of his rosary were slipping through his fingers. He was muttering a prayer. The only salvation lies in prayer, thought Polzer, fervent prayer for hours on end.

'What do you want?' asked Karl in a hoarse voice. 'Put the knife down. Are you going to kill me? I'll scream. What have I done to you? Help! Help!'

'You said something,' said Polzer.

The nurse's muttering stopped.

'What did I say? Did I say I murdered her? Did I say that? Don't believe him, Herr Sonntag. I didn't say anything. He's the murderer, it can't have been anyone else. And take that head away. Call the police. Get it over with. Throw the head out into the street so people will come. Help! help!'

The nurse stood up.

'You said something,' said Polzer.

'Said, said! Stay, Herr Sonntag, I didn't say any-thing. That I haven't got any legs, that's what I said. That someone might kill me, I said. That you're as stupid as a calf, I said. Put the knife down, you're the murderer.'

'Confess,' said the nurse, 'that you did it for her money.'

Polzer dropped the knife. He sank to his knees. 'Help me,' he said.

Karl was silent.

The nurse came over to Karl's chair. Eyes wide, Karl watched him come. 'Stay here!' he screamed. 'Stay! I won't help him. Why should I help him? Stay!'

The bell rang.

'With your permission,' said the nurse with a bow, 'I'll go and let Frau Fanta in. I'll show her into the next room. This might well be too much for the lady.'

Karl bent forward a long way. Spittle was dribbling out of his mouth. 'Run!' he said. 'Run for it! I can't speak. He'll kill me as well. I know who threw the head onto the stairs. It's all been worked out, right down to the last detail. Off you go! Run for it!'

Yes, yes, thought Polzer, he must flee. He had to get away from there. They all hated him. And Franz wasn't coming, either. He had to go back. He had to stand in the shop once more and see his aunt's parting. He had to bear things to the very end, he thought. That is the way things are for us.

The nurse came back in. Dora could be heard sobbing in the next room. Polzer got up off his knees. He turned and slowly walked towards the door.

Karl watched him go.

'I'm going,' said Polzer.

Karl sat up. He twisted and turned in the restraining straps, making his chair shift. 'No!' he screamed, 'No! You can't go, Polzer, you can't leave me alone, Polzer! I'll be for it next. Stay, stay, don't leave me alone with this . . .'

'With your permission,' Sonntag, the nurse, interrupted in calm, insistent tones. 'Perhaps I should leave you alone with Herr Polzer. That seems to me the more agreeable solution.'

Karl was breathing audibly. His forehead was damp with sweat. The nurse took off his apron and wrapped it round the knife. He went with silent footsteps to the door of his room.

'I will say goodbye to Frau Fanta. It is a matter of courtesy. I am familiar with the demands of polite behaviour. Cover the head with a towel, Herr Polzer.'

He bowed and silently closed the door behind him.

Karl's head had fallen to one side. He was motionless. He seemed to have lost consciousness.

APPENDIX

The following was originally written as the final chapter of The Maimed, *but omitted by Ungar from the published version. It was printed – without reference to the novel – in the literary periodical* Vers und Prosa 1924, *vol 1, part 5, pp 177–180. Clearly Ungar decided to keep the identity of the murderer a mystery.*

The doctor heard rapid footsteps behind him. Someone caught up with him. The nurse was standing before him

The doctor took a step back. 'Murderer,' he said, 'murderer!'

'That's all over,' said the nurse. He was carrying his package under his arm.

'Nothing is over,' cried the doctor. 'There'll be a new trial. Now I see it clearly. You dominated them all. The truth must be brought to light. You must be arrested. At once, today.'

'The truth will not come to light,' said the nurse. 'Whenever it becomes visible, it is already distorted and defiled. Polzer has been acquitted. What more do you want? More unhappiness? Herr Fanta, Dora and Kamilla sent to prison for perjury? Who would thank you for that? Or is it the crime and its atonement that concerns you? What do we know of that?'

'What do we know of that? Murderer, murderer!' exclaimed the doctor.

Sonntag, the nurse, was silent for a moment before

going on. He spoke calmly, as always. 'You see me for the last time, doctor. I am not going back to Herr Fanta's any more. My way has come to an end there. Now once again it is time to continue my tireless search for Christ elsewhere. Perhaps some night, as you are leaving Herr Fanta's house, you will hear echoing footsteps and see the dark figure of a man disappear round the corner. I have the feeling I will often be standing at night outside the house where the widow Porges was murdered. Perhaps you'll be sitting up there and the conversation will suddenly fall silent.'

'We'll find you, catch you,' said the doctor.

'They will not catch me because they will not look for me. And if they should look for me, no one will find me. Tomorrow morning I will have another name, I will be one of the hundreds of thousands in the tenements. My way has not yet come to its end.'

'They must find you! They must put you in irons! What did you do to those women? To all of them. And are still doing, even today? The sufferings you have made that poor Polzer go through! And now, why are you here before me? What do you want? Murderer. Murderer!'

The nurse looked at him in silence. Then he said, 'I am waiting for you to call for help. To shout for the police. But you are not shouting. You know that it is not my destiny, yet. I do not fear the judgments of earthly judges. Everything must be atoned for in Christ, and now I have atoned for the dreadful murder of the Prossnitz nun. But as long as we are here, there is no end to atonement, and there is no atonement which will erase the deed from our hearts. We approach, but the way is eternal before our soul is with Christ.'

'Christ! Christ! Silence, blasphemer!'

'It is true that I blaspheme God, for I should not speak His name. But I am on the path to Him, though distant. It was destined that I should commit the crime against the nun.'

'Against the nun?'

'I murdered her, the one I was talking about. I lay in bed with broken limbs. But I was strong, and my hatred was strong, and I killed her with my knife in God-denying hatred and violated her. But then God arose within me, and I came tumbling down in Him, and I spent the days in prayer to obliterate myself, I scourged myself with rods, I confessed and did penance and began to serve the sick, to bind their wounds and clean them of stinking pus, and in the night I called out to God that I recognised Christ and that I desired forgiveness, and all the time I bore my sin like a gaping wound in my breast. Until I came to understand that there is only one atonement and that it is eternal atonement and that there is no comfort beside that, only pain and Christian remorse beside that, and that this is atonement: to incline yourself once more to the crime you committed out of hatred, but with Christ in your heart, with love and humility, to commit it again in Christ, against Him, whom your heart loves and seeks and who is clear of sin, to push Him away with your wrong-doing, for Christ's sake humbly to immerse yourself in all the anguish of your crime once more, to become a murderer once more, stretching up your blood-stained hands for grace like a drowning man, Lord, for there are no words, no devotion, no remorse, there is only the deed, the sinful deed committed again as atonement, it is there and we can never erase it, we have to suffer it, again and again, thus confessing our love for Christ, the blessed, the pure, and His mother Mary in her sorrows, who veil their faces in tears and turn away from us in our sorrows, for the way to Him is eternal, we come no nearer to Him, we keep pushing Him farther away, and that is the way we must seek.'

It seemed to the doctor that the nurse's eyes were flickering. He did not dare speak.

'And now that the sacrifice is made,' said the nurse, 'I will go. I am a murderer, you say, woe is me, I am a murderer! But that I suffer for Christ's sake, that I seek Him with the blood of my heart, in the blood of my sins, my beyond atonement sins, my eternal atonement, for Christ, for Him whom I love, do you believe that?'

He stood facing the doctor, right in front of him. His voice was trembling. He was looking at the doctor. The doctor did not know whether he was pleading or threatening. But he was waiting.

'Yes . . .' said the doctor falteringly, 'I . . . believe you.'

At that Sonntag seized the doctor's hand and, falling to the rain-soaked ground, kissed it. The doctor tried to pull his hand away, but Sonntag had already sprung to his feet and was disappearing in the darkness, in the direction from which he had come.

The doctor stood there, motionless, watching him go. 'What . . . are you going . . . to do,' he said.

I ought to run after him and arrest him, thought the doctor. He's a murderer. He'll be laughing at me, he'll be thinking I won't do anything to harm him any more, now he's kissed my hand. Perhaps that's what he's thinking. He's a murderer. An insane murderer.'

The rain was getting heavier. He shivered. He did not have a coat on.